*Ev*

# Giovanni

By

# Eve Vaughn

## Dedication

To my readers who have supported me throughout my journey in completing this series. Thank you so much for supporting me, and keeping me going. I hope you'll enjoy reading this book as much as I've enjoyed writing it.

Thank you Shayna and Wanda for holding things down for me when things get a little crazy in my life.

Thanks Mom for loving my books.

And Thanks to my Dad just because.

This is a work of fiction. Names, characters, places, and incidents are products of the author's imagination or are used fictitiously and are not to be construed as real. Any resemblance to actual events, locales, organizations, or persons living or dead is entirely coincidental.

All trademarks, service marks, registered service marks are the property of their respective owners and are used herein for identification purposes only.

## Prologue

"Are you sure you want to do this?" Steel stared at him with a shrewd narrowed gaze, as if trying to get a proper read on Giovanni's state of mind.

Giovanni made sure to keep his thoughts firmly locked away from the warlock's scrutiny. No one understood the dangers of this process more than him but this was something that needed to happen. For the past few centuries he'd taken up the dark arts in order to protect his family. He'd tried his best to use the magic sparingly but each time he did, he could feel it consume a part of him. There were times when his mind would completely slip away and he wasn't himself. The blackouts and the need to kill and destroy, which had once been few and far between, were more frequent occurrences.

He was turning rogue.

Without the purge it wouldn't be long before he became the monster he'd been fighting against all these years. He'd only began to practice black magic to combat his mother and older brother who had been practicing it for years. He needed it to keep them at bay and protect those who were at the time not old or strong enough to protect themselves. He had hoped that with these powers he could somehow defeat his mother and save his brothers. All of them. But one thing he discovered after he took up the dark arts was that one didn't use such a force, it used you. He'd become its slave for half a millennium. It had been a daily struggle to hold on to his identity when it was clear that it had already consumed the one brother who needed saving the most.

Finally he nodded in response to the warlock's question. "Yes."

Steel Romanov raised a brow. "You've utilized black magic longer than most without losing your sanity which is no easy feat. It has essentially become a part of you. To separate you from it now could kill you."

"I'm fully aware of the possible consequences. I knew the danger before I approached you. I also understood the price I had to pay in order to possess this power. If the cost of getting rid of it is my life then so be it. I would rather die than to have another life on my conscience."

"Okay. We'll do this now." Steel nodded toward his brothers who were also in attendance. The two identical warlocks stepped forward. "In order to perform such a spell, it will take all three of us. I won't go through the details of how this works because I'm sure you've already done your research. But once we start this there's no changing your mind."

Giovanni bowed his head in assent. "Of course."

Cutter placed a hand on Giovanni's shoulder. "And you know of the other....after effects?"

"Besides the fact that this spell could kill me? There's something else besides that?"

Blade cleared his throat. "There are things worse than death."

Giovanni looked at each of the brothers and wondered what they weren't telling him. "What else I should know?"

Steel paused before answering. "The purification spell could kill you it's true, but you're quite old so your chances are good of surviving it. Besides death, this spell can also render you mortal. It's my understanding that it could be temporary but it's quite possible you'll never be a vampire again. So I ask you again, are you sure you want to go through with this?"

"Whether I survive this or not it's a death sentence. I could either die now or of old age," he mused more to himself than to the others in the room. He didn't fear death. In fact he'd danced with it so many times over the past centuries that perhaps it was time to give his old friend a proper greeting. But before he finally met his maker there was one thing he had to do and that was to fulfill his promise to a friend. In order to do that he needed to cleanse himself of the evil that threatened to consume his soul.

Concern etched lines in Steel's otherwise ageless face. "The decision is yours."

The thought of finally finding peace was too much of a temptation to resist. "Yes. Go ahead and do it. I'm ready…no matter the consequences."

# Chapter One

"The surgery should have restored your sight. This is the third procedure since your accident and each one has been a failure. I had pinned my hopes on this last one because it's so new and innovative but unfortunately, if you haven't noticed a difference by now it's not likely there will be any. I'm sorry Ms. Lewis, but I'm afraid that the probability is you'll never see again."

Sydney bit her bottom lip to hold back a cry. She'd been told before the surgery that her chances were 50/50 for a full or even partial recovery of sight but she had decided to go ahead with the procedure anyway. Never being one to live with "what ifs", Sydney figured there was no harm in trying. She was already blind so there was no risk in losing vision she didn't have. Though she'd prepared herself for this news, she couldn't help but feel a stab of disappointment cutting through her heart. She promised herself she wouldn't get emotional if it was bad news.

"Ms. Lewis," Dr. Wyncote began before breaking into a series of coughs. "Excuse me. Do you have any questions for me?"

She shook her head. "Not really. It's just...I thought...well, when the bandages were removed shortly after the surgery, I saw light again and then shadows; I still do but it hasn't improved beyond that. You'd told me then that it was a good sign."

"That's true, which is why I'm surprised no progress has been made."

"So, there's no more hope? Nothing else that can be done?"

A pregnant pause commenced before Dr. Wyncote answered. "I've consulted with my colleagues and even shared your charts with a few of the top ophthalmological surgeons in the country and believe me, if there was anything else I believed could be done, I'd be the first to inform you of it. But unfortunately there isn't. Now, you're welcome to get another opinion, and I encourage all my patients to do so if they're not satisfied with my professional judgment, but I honestly think it will be a waste of your time. Keep in mind, I'm not the first surgeon you've consulted on this matter."

Sydney bowed her head in defeat. No matter how much she'd prepared herself for this possibility it was still hard to reconcile. She'd been blind for that last ten years of her life but even as she relearned to live her life in darkness, there had always been that one thing that had kept her going. Hope. To relinquish it now was almost like losing an old friend. The fiery sting of tears burned her eyes but she refused to shed them. Not here. Not now.  ·

Sydney took a deep calming breath before she could trust herself to speak. "You're right, doctor. We did speak of this being a possibility before and I had prepared myself for the worst case scenario, but I guess hearing it in my mind versus hearing it in reality are two different things." She let out a humorless snort.

"Ms. Lewis, I can understand your disappointment. It's only natural because you're human. I'll admit that I feel a bit let down as well because you seemed like the perfect candidate for this procedure. I hate giving my patients bad news and I'd hoped this outcome would be different."

"I know it's not your fault. You've been great and I appreciate everything you've done for me. If it weren't for you, I wouldn't know about half the programs available for a person with my disability. I've been able to live a mostly normal life."

"It's been my pleasure, Ms. Lewis. On the bright side, you seem to have adjusted admirably. You're independent and seem to be navigating your life quite well."

Sydney shrugged. "Well, as independent as I can be. I'll never drive a car or see a proper sunset again, but hey, I guess I'm just lucky to be alive." She didn't mean to be so self-deprecating, but the thought of missing out on the beautiful colors in the world and being able to read a person's expression, or even just seeing the way the leaves rustled in the wind flayed at her spirit.

The scrapping of chair legs against the floor alerted Sydney that Dr. Wyncote was now standing. The soft foot falls against the carpet's floor got louder before a heavy hand fell on her shoulder. "I know you're trying to be brave, but it's okay to be emotional now. Here's a tissue."

She reached out and encountered his other hand which was only inches away from her face before taking the offered tissue. Perhaps it was the gentleness of his tone that was her undoing, but the tears she'd valiantly tried to hold back came bursting forth like a flood. She'd never allowed herself the indulgence to cry over her disability because the same time she'd lost her vision was also when she'd lost her family.

Her life had not been anything out of the ordinary. She'd been a normal 19-year old home for the summer from her first year of college. She had a job at a local grocery store as a cashier in order to have a little extra spending money for her next semester in school. She remembered that day clearly. She'd worked a double shift and her feet had been killing her. After clocking out and leaving to catch the bus home, she was met in the parking lot by her parents and her sister. Her father had decided to take the family out to dinner that night and had wanted to surprise Sydney after her shift.

Sydney couldn't remember a time when she'd enjoyed her family more. She and her younger sister Tara had looked on with smug expressions as their father had ordered the largest steak on the menu with the knowledge he'd be on the couch later with his top button undone and groaning that he was dying. Their mother just silently shook her head and muttered under her breath about him needing an antacid for later. The family had talked and laughed together and Sydney just looked on at them thinking how lucky she was to be a part of this loving group of people. None of them were perfect, herself included, but they were hers.

On the way home they'd stopped for ice cream and by the time they headed home Sydney had been truly stuffed and having worked all day, she'd drifted off to sleep in the car. The next thing she remembered was being jolted awake by the sound of an ear piercing scream—her mother's. After that she'd felt the sensation of being violently jostled. The very last thing she saw before passing out was Tara's bloody face.

It was still a vision that haunted her dreams although when she was awake, she was mostly surrounded by darkness. When the doctor had come by her bedside, she couldn't understand why she wasn't able to see. The news that she'd lost her sight however didn't compare to the pain of knowing her parents and sister hadn't survived the car crash. Apparently some teenagers had been joyriding and had lost control of their vehicle before plowing into her father's car, shoving it into a busy intersection where it was hit three more times by oncoming cars. It didn't make Sydney feel better to learn that they could have all possibly survived were it not for the last impact of a box truck or that the teenagers didn't survive either.

Though she'd gone through the motions of having some semblance of a life after such a major loss, it had been difficult. Had it not been for the help of close family friends and people in her small town rallying around her, Sydney didn't know how she'd make it through. Now ten years later, she felt that she was in a place in her life where she was content. She still missed her family desperately, but in the last ten years she'd managed to pull her life together and live independently. She'd learned to function with her disability and managed to handle herself well. Of course she relied on the help of others at times, but she didn't know a single person in the world who didn't require any help at all.

Sydney ran a boarding house which enabled her to pay her bills and to do something she loved which was playing music. She had friends, and loved taking on new adventures that most sighted people would be scared to try. Her life was fulfilling in a way she never thought it would be again, but her vision had always been something she believed she'd eventually regain. Now hearing that it was just an elusive dream, Sydney was crushed.

Dr. Wyncote tugged Sydney out of her seat and pulled her into his tight embrace. His thick arms were warm and comforting as she sobbed even more releasing years of frustration. "It's going to be okay. I have every faith in you that you'll do well."

Though his words were meant to be reassuring they only served to make her cry even harder. She released all her pent-up emotions until her head ached and her eyes couldn't produce anymore tears. Her entire body felt as if it had been plowed over by a bulldozer by the time she finished. Feeling physically exhausted, she practically wilted against her surgeon's body.

He gently guided her back to her chair. "I'm so sorry," he murmured.

Sydney sniffed. "You don't have to apologize. It's not your fault," she managed to get out. Her throat was sore and raw.

"Is there anyone out in the waiting to room to take you home?"

She blew her nose into the tissue she'd been clutching for dear life before answering. "No. I took the bus." Sydney tapped the side of her watch.

*It is 3:09 PM*, its electronic voice informed.

"Looks like my bus will be here in twenty minutes. I should get going."

"Actually, you're my last appointment for the day and I have no surgeries scheduled. I thought I'd take the remainder of the day off. I'd be happy to give you a ride home."

She shook her head vehemently. Sydney was certain he didn't offer rides to his other patients. He probably only did it out of pity. The last thing she wanted was for someone to feel sorry for her. She'd fought too hard for her independence for people to offer help simply because they felt bad for the poor blind woman. "Thank you but I prefer to ride to the bus. Besides I don't want to take you out of your way."

"Well, if you're sure."

Sydney couldn't keep the smirk from twisting her lips. She noticed he didn't insist. Just as she suspected, he'd only offered her a ride to assuage some sense of guilt he probably felt. "I am. But thank you again. I should get going if I want to catch my bus on time." She gathered her purse and cane and headed out the door.

Once she was out of the medical building, she released a heavy sigh as she raised her head to the sun. Though she could perceive the light, she couldn't see the sky or the clouds. When she was little, her mom would yell at her, saying Sydney would ruin her eyes because she liked to stare directly at the sun. It had been her wish that she'd get a chance to see that beautiful star one more time.

But now she'd only ever see it in her dreams.

Giovanni looked at the rusted number 127 on the weather-beaten mailbox that looked like it had seen better days. This was it. Ahead of him on a narrow dirt path rested a large white Victorian house with a screened-in porch. The expanse of green lawn it rested on was neatly manicured. On either side of the structure were large oak trees, one of which was sporting a tire swing. Despite the chipped paint and a couple of shutters hanging from the hinges, the house had a certain Southern charm that seemed to lend itself to lazy picnics on the lawn, or simply sitting on the steps sipping an ice cold drink under the unforgiving heat of the sun.

This would be his home for the next few months, or at least however long he was needed. He'd only studied this place from afar, and caught its owner from a distance, but now that he was actually here, he couldn't bring himself to move toward the front door. He wasn't sure what kept him rooted in the spot. No. He knew exactly why. Once he entered that house there would be no turning back. No matter what happened his fate would be sealed. The question was, could he handle it? Could she? Part of him wanted to turn, run and never look back, but he'd made a promise. And after all the shit he'd done in the past, he had a lot to atone for.

Squaring his shoulders, Giovanni took a deep breath and made the trek up the dirt path, moving as slowly as he possibly could. Once at the screen door, however, he noticed for the first time that the porch was occupied. He wasn't sure why he hadn't seen the woman initially. Before he'd undergone the spell, her presence wouldn't have gone unnoticed. But then again, there were a lot of things different about him now. He was still trying to get accustomed to the new man he'd become.

The old woman rocked back and forth in an oversized rocking chair that seemed to engulf her body. Lines intersected all over her sun-darkened skin, giving her the look of someone who'd lived many years. Her iron gray hair was pulled back in a severe bun, and the wrinkles around her mouth made it look puckered and a little mean. She stared at him with eyes small and dark like onyx, and it almost seemed as if she was staring right though him. There was a time when he could listen to the beat of a person's heart and could tell by how strongly it beat how old that person was. His extraordinary sense of hearing was another casualty of the spell.

Her blank expression gave nothing away. Giovanni hesitated for a moment, waiting for the woman to speak, but when she didn't he shifted on his feet nervously. He cleared his throat, unsure of himself for the first time since he could remember. "Uh, I'm looking for a Miss Sydney Lewis."

The woman stared at him blankly, still not saying a word.

"This is her house, isn't it?" He knew for a fact that it was but he wanted the verbal conformation so he could continue on with his task.

She continued to rock silently.

Perhaps the woman was deaf. "Is Sydney Lewis home?" he practically yelled the words.

The woman flared her nostrils and practically sneered. "I may be an old woman, but I hear perfectly fine." The cadence in her voice was slow and sharp, blunting the charm of her southern lilt.

The little bit of patience he had been holding on to was gone. He raised a brow. "Then I'm sure you heard me the first time."

She eyed the bag he carried with him. It was a plain canvas duffle bag chosen because it was inconspicuous, unlike the expensive luggage he could easily afford. "I suppose you're looking to stay."

Giovanni had scouted this place from a distance and wasn't familiar with this woman. She was a probably another boarder but she certainly possessed an air of a woman who claimed whatever domain she resided in. "This is a boarding house, isn't it? I spoke to Miss Lewis on the phone and she's expecting me."

"I help her run this place. Can't say I remember her mentioning a new person coming this week."

He never realized how much he'd taken his powers for granted. In a former life, he would have glamored her. The old woman would be eating out the palm of his hands but he was just an ordinary man. No special abilities and with an infinite amount of frustration.

15

Giovanni mentally counted down ten and released a sigh. "Perhaps it slipped her mind but I informed her I'd be here today."

The woman narrowed her eyes. "I doubt it. Sydney tells me everything."

"I'm sorry, Ms. — I didn't catch your name."

"Because I didn't throw it."

He bit his tongue to hold back a curse. Before he could think of a calm response, he heard the soft sounds of footsteps approaching. He turned to see a tall dark-skinned woman in a yellow sundress approach. His heart skipped several beats as his breath caught in his throat. It had been several months since he'd last seen her and never this close.

She was tall and curvaceous, reminding him of a Botticelli painting come to life. Her eyes were large, framed with long thick lashes while her lips were full and pouty. Proud cheek bones rested in a face that Giovanni believed was complete perfection. She wore her hair cropped closely to her scalp, but the look suited her. It brought the focus to her angelic face. Her dress, which wouldn't be considered risqué on most bodies, was absolutely sinful on hers, particularly for the way it skimmed her generous hips and breasts.

He'd almost forgotten the way she'd made him feel the first time he'd seen her. But as she drew closer his ability to speak or even think had faded away. All he could see was her and how the sun glistened off of her beautiful brown skin that reminded him of silken sable.

As if his feet had a mind of their own, they began to move, propelling him toward her. He reached out when she was arm's length in front of him and touched her arm. The beauty gasped, her gorgeous brown eyes widening in surprise as a jolt of electricity shot through his body.

Suddenly darkness consumed him as he experienced the sensation of falling.

## Chapter Two

Sydney didn't see the stranger fall, but she'd certainly heard the heavy drop of his body to the ground. She knelt down and reached out for him. It was ice cold! She yanked her hand away, fearing the worst. No, this couldn't be happening. His body wouldn't have lost heat so quickly. She reached out again and found his chest and then moved her hand along his solid frame until she found his neck. There was a pulse, but it was slow.

"Ida!" she called out, hoping her friend was on the porch or at least looking out from the kitchen window.

"No need to yell, I'm here, child."

Sydney could hear the faint creaking of Ida's favorite rocking chair in the background and assumed she'd been there all along. "I think we need to call an ambulance. He passed out."

"Maybe he's been out in the sun too long. Carolina summers are usually pretty mild but this year it's been a beast."

"I don't think he's suffering from heatstroke, he's not warm. He's the opposite, actually." She pressed her head on his forehead which felt clammy. He hadn't spoken before he'd touched her and he didn't wear any identifying colognes which would have helped identify him, although he did have a clean, after-shower scent mingled with a masculine fragrance that was uniquely his.

When he'd made contact with her, she felt a jolt she couldn't explain. It was the sensation of being shocked by someone who wore wool socks rubbing them against the carpet, but much more intense. She couldn't quite explain it beyond that.

And now he lay at her feet, apparently passed out, and she didn't understand what was happening. Her earlier visit to the doctor's office was pushed to the back of her mind as she focused her attention on this stranger.

"I still think we should get him some medical attention. Could you make that call?" She spoke in Ida's general direction.

"Why don't you try to rouse him before getting anyone else involved? He doesn't look that terribly sick to me. Maybe a little pale. Could be a junkie. We don't need that kind of trouble around here."

Sydney frowned. It wasn't like Ida to be so unhelpful. "Why would you think that? Who is he anyway?"

"Someone claiming to be a new boarder. Said he talked to you on the phone."

Sydney smacked her forehead. "Oh, no. I've been so worried about my appointment that I forgot to mention we'd be getting a new boarder this week. He said he'd be here tomorrow but there was a possibility that he would show up today. I can't believe it slipped my mind. I had the agency run his information, of course, and everything seemed to check out. His name is John Chandler."

"Hmph," Ida grunted. "There's something about this guy I don't quite trust."

Just then, John stirred with a groan. "Sydney," he whispered her name like a soft caress, sending another wave of awareness shooting through her body. She could feel his gaze on her which seemed to burn a hole in her skin. She wasn't sure why she would react to a stranger this way but it made her more than a little uncomfortable.

"Yes. Are you Mr. Chandler?"

"*Mi scusi?*"

"I'm sorry?"

"Umm, yes. I am he. But please, John will do."

"You frightened me, passing out like that. Should we call you an ambulance? This sun has been a killer lately."

"No. Please don't."

"Are you sure? You gave us a bit of a scare."

"Trust me. I'll be fine. Actually, I'm just exhausted. I've been awake for a while."

"Hmm, well, if you're sure."

"I am."

"Well in that case, you're in luck, even though I didn't think you'd show up until tomorrow, we have a room for you. Ida can show you to your room. We can discuss rules and what not after you've rested. You'll have to accept my apologies because I'm just getting home from an appointment." She realized she was babbling and laughed nervously.

Sydney scooted away from him and reached for her cane before wobbling to her feet.

"The only room that's ready is Dylan's room." Ida huffed the words, seeming very put out that Sydney would dare offer the one room in the house that remained vacant.

"It's the only room that's clean and ready for a guest. Mr. Chandler — er, John can stay there for the night and we'll prepare one for him for the remainder of his stay if that's okay with you, Ida." Sydney added that last part without bothering to disguise her annoyance. She couldn't figure out what had gotten into her friend, who didn't seem to like their new guest.

Mr. Chandler shuffled on the ground. Sydney figured he was attempting to get up. She would have offered him a hand for leverage but was too scared to make contact with him again. She could tell when he was on his feet again, because he had somehow invaded her space and the warmth of his breath gently flowed against her lips.

"Well, I suppose if you're going to stay then I might as well show you to your room," Ida grumbled ungraciously.

Sydney would definitely have to find out what was going on with the older woman when they got some time alone.

"Well, I look forward to talking to you later." Mr. Chandler spoke.

"Likewise," Sydney answered to be polite. She got along with most of her boarders, some whom she'd even become quite close to over the years, but there was something about this man that made her feel emotions she couldn't quite understand and that made him dangerous.

It was only when he finally walked away from her did Sydney release the breath she didn't realize she'd been holding. They'd spoken briefly on the phone and from what she gathered, he was basically a drifter who traveled a lot and wanted to spend a little time in the South and see some sights. He said he was willing to pay for three months stay upfront.

Since her accident, she hadn't had much luck with dating so she'd given up on ever finding a love. For some reason she seemed to attract men who either fetishized her condition or the ones who babied her and wouldn't let her do the most mundane of tasks. She could do without either types of men and was happy with her life without being fussed over all the time. Like most hot-blooded women, she did miss the companionship of a lover and there were times when she was lonely. She'd tried to just do the casual thing with a couple guys, hang out with no strings attached and fulfill each other's needs. But both situations had turned out to be disasters with each of the men falling into the two category of guys she tried to avoid. Now it was just her and her trusted vibrator. And if she ever got lonely, she'd call a friend to hang out.

Sydney wondered what Mr. Chandler looked like. He seemed tall and his voice was deep and sexy. She detected a faint accent. She didn't miss the fact that he'd slipped and spoke another language which sounded like Spanish or Italian. Maybe he was born in another country. She couldn't be sure. She bet he looked as good as he sounded.

"Get it together, girl," she muttered to herself. He was her boarder. Nothing more. All these thoughts of this new guy reminded her to replace the batteries in her dildo. She had a feeling it would be a long night.

Sydney started to wash the few dishes that still lingered in the sink. She didn't want to dwell on her earlier appointment or her new housemate. Sydney heard Ida's heavy sigh when she entered the kitchen.

Ida grumbled something Sydney didn't quite catch before rummaging through the pots and pans. "Guess I might as well start dinner. Looks like I'm going to need to stretch the meal for an extra person."

Sydney couldn't figure out why her friend seemed to be so put out by the new boarder. Sure Ida had the type of personality that took some getting used to, and she could be gruff at times, but for the most part she was harmless. Ida also had a heart of gold. "Look, Ida, I'm sorry for not mentioning him earlier. I guess with everything going on, it clearly slipped my mind."

"This is your house and who you invite in to it is none of my business."

"Maybe so, but we both know you're invaluable here and your opinion matters to me. Clearly there's something about this situation you don't like."

There was a long pause as Ida seemed to busy herself with the tasks of preparing dinner. For a moment Sydney didn't think the older woman would answer, but finally Ida sighed. "Perhaps I'm just being foolish and set in my ways but there's something about that man I don't trust. How much do you know about him?"

"About as much as I know about any of the other boarders. He passed the background check. Decent credit, no criminal history. And he was willing to pay for the first three months plus the deposit in advance. He's already wired the money to the broker so I could hardly turn him away. Besides, the extra money won't hurt. It could go to some of the much needed repairs."

"We would have gotten by. But I guess it doesn't matter. He's here now and there's not much I can do about it. I just wish you wouldn't have offered him Dylan's room. He'll be coming back soon."

A cold chill ran down Sydney's spine at the mention of Ida's grandson. He wasn't exactly Sydney's favorite person. He was arrogant, short-tempered and often rude to the other boarders. When he was around Sydney would bite her tongue to keep the peace. She mostly tolerated him for Ida's sake, even going as far as letting him stay at the house whenever he was in town. He worked for a construction company that did a lot of work out of town, so fortunately he wasn't around that much.

"You said he wouldn't be back for a few more days so it shouldn't be a problem for John to stay in Dylan's room. And by tomorrow we'll have another spot ready for him. I understand you're a little wary about the new guy but if he causes any problems or violates the house rules, he'll be evicted."

"Well, it's *your* house. I have no say in anything. It's not like my input matters much."

Sydney sighed, backing away from the sink and walking towards Ida's voice. She reached out and felt for Ida's shoulder. "Ida, you know I value your opinion. Your friendship means more to me than you know. I couldn't run this place without you. So let's not argue about this, okay? How about I help you with dinner when I finish the rest of the dishes?"

Ida patted Sydney on the cheek. "You're a good girl, Sydney. I just worry about you is all. But if you are okay with this then so am I. And no, you don't have to help me with dinner. It's all under control. I already have a chicken marinating on the counter. I just need to pre-heat the oven first."

"Okay." Sydney went back to her task at the sink.

"You never told me how your appointment went."

Sydney hunched over and willed herself not to get emotional. She'd already done enough crying in the doctor's office. She refused to start up again. "I'd prepared myself for the worse but I'm still a little disappointed."

"The operation wasn't successful, I take it?"

"No. The thing is, I was so sure that my sight was coming back after the procedure. I could see shadows and could make out shapes. That's the best I'd seen in years. But then nothing again. I don't know what happened. Anyway, Dr. Wyncote seemed as surprised as I was that it wasn't a success. He believed with the immediate progress after the surgery that it was a promising sign that I'd regain some or if not all of my vision back. But with the last setback, he doesn't think there's anything else that can be done."

"Well, we did discuss all possibilities and you knew this was one of them. I know you're disappointed, child, but you're going to be okay. You navigate this world better than most sighted people. My old eyes aren't much better."

"But at least your old eyes can see. I get that you're trying to comfort me, but can we change the subject? I don't want to talk about this anymore." Sydney snorted. It wasn't her intention to be rude but the last thing she needed right now was to be patronized.

"Of course, but just know that you're strong. You'll get through this."

"I'll tell you what. I'll finish these dishes and you go lay down. I'm sure you're tired after the long day you've had."

"That's okay. I need something to do to keep me occupied."

"If that's what you think is best."

Sydney returned her focus on her task and Ida seemed to do the same. They worked in silence during which time, Sydney's mind kept drifting to the mysterious John Chandler.

## Chapter Three

Nya watched the family from a distance, debating on whether she should approach. They looked happy. The little boy chased his younger sister, threatening to tickle her. She was saved, however, when the children's father joined them and swooped the girl off her feet and spun her around. She laughed and squealed with delight. "Faster, Daddy!" she screamed.

As this scene took place, the mother snapped pictures on a camera most professionals would envy. They were the perfect family. They might not have been traditional in appearance, with a white father, an Asian mother and two African-America children, but there was nothing untraditional about the obvious love the four subjects of Nya's observation felt for each other. To those not in the know, no one would ever guess that the parents were also vampires with the father being quite old.

A twinge of envy tore at Nya's breast. She didn't begrudge this family their happiness, but she was jealous of the ease in which they were able to give and receive love to each other. It was an emotion she didn't think she was capable of. Sure, she cared deeply for the few people she called friend, but she wasn't sure if that was love. She didn't know what love was anymore. She'd spent several decades denying that emotion and when she finally acknowledged it, it was too late. And now that fleeting feeling was gone forever, leaving her with a numbness that consumed every part of her.

When she ate, she couldn't taste the food. She partook in blood but didn't give her the heady rush that it once had. When she fucked, she felt nothing. Nya feared this would be her life for as long as she walked the Earth. The fact that she was immortal meant that living like that was a curse.

She had no right to be here, watching this family behind the shadows so she wouldn't be detected. She kept herself at a distance far enough to not be detected, knowing that if the older vampire wasn't so occupied with his family he might have noticed the presence of another immortal in the vicinity.

Slowly, she backed away as she silently wished them a farewell. She departed with a heavy sigh and contemplated where her next destination would be. Hopefully the next place she wouldn't run into anyone she knew, and in particular two very determined adversaries who dogged her heels. She contemplated checking on Giovanni to see how he was handling the task she'd given to him. She hadn't heard from him in weeks but she knew by now that he should be nestled in the small little town in South Carolina. She was certain he'd take care of the little problem down there. He'd never let her down before and she didn't expect him to now.

Once she assured herself that things would be handled, Nya slid into her vehicle and drove off into obscurity.

*Giovanni sat by the pond and sullenly threw rocks into the water to watch it ripple. It had a calming effect on him. His*

chest hurt but he refused to cry. Men didn't cry, and even if no one was watching he wouldn't allow himself this indulgence. No matter how hard he tried to impress his father, nothing seemed to please him. If he did well with his tutors it didn't matter. Any attempt to impress Don Sarducci with his knowledge of the land or anything Giovanni believed would be of interest was met with failure. In fact, his father who seemed to be irritated by his presence, would often scold him for things his brother would get praised for. He'd be lying to himself if he didn't acknowledge the twinge of jealousy he felt toward Adonis, the favored son.

It was Adonis whom his father would take on horseback rides along their massive estate. Adonis would be treated to exotic gifts from their father's travels. If Giovanni was given anything it was usually an afterthought and nowhere near as grand as anything Adonis received. Still, Giovanni was grateful for any crumbs his father threw his way, which were few and far between. Despite this he loved his brother, who looked out for him when their father was being particularly critical.

Giovanni had no doubt that if he dropped dead today, his father wouldn't bat an eye. His mama was no better. The only time she paid any attention to him was in front of guests where she pretended to actually care. Most other times, she simply ignored his presence.

"I thought I'd find you in the stables talking to that boy again."

Giovanni looked up to see his brother standing over him.

"That boy is older than us."

Adonis shrugged. "So? He's a servant. Does it really matter?"

Giovanni hated when his brother took on such an arrogant tone but he dismissed it. His mind was on other things. "Our father says that I've been spending too much time with the help and it's unbecoming of his son." It was true he spent a lot of time with the stable master's assistant. His father ran a strict household and was particularly hard on the servants. Most of them were too scared to look the family members in the eyes let alone speak to them unless spoken to, but not Gio, his namesake. It was him who Giovanni would run to whenever his father said something cruel or made him feel worthless. Gio always had good advice and whenever Giovanni spoke to him, he felt better. He felt an affinity toward the stable worker that he couldn't quite explain. It was like there was some kind of intangible connection between them.

Silly as it may have been, he often wished Gio was his real father. The Don certainly wasn't much as one. Unfortunately for him, one of the other servants apparently reported how much time Giovanni was spending in the stables with Gio. He'd received a tongue-lashing along with ten strikes to the back with his father's cane. It had curtailed his visits but didn't stop them. He couldn't stay away and refused to be parted from the only father figure he had.

"The stable master sent him to town on an errand."

Adonis lowered himself to the ground to sit next to Giovanni. "It's a good thing. Papa says you spend too much time with that man. You're lucky he hasn't had the man whipped."

"For what? Being kind to me when my own father treats me with contempt?" He might only be ten but he was old enough to know how his sire felt toward him.

Adonis sighed. "Papa cares for you, he just doesn't know how to show it."

"He has no problems showing you. If you've come out here to defend him like you always do, then I don't want to hear it." Giovanni stood up and threw another rock into the pond with all his might."

"I didn't. I came out here to see how you're doing. It wasn't fair that you would be punished for such a minor indiscretion. I told Papa this. He's willing to hear you out."

29

*While his brother was willing to dismiss the incident as inconsequential, Giovanni didn't see it that way. "They were starving. What did you expect me to do?"*

*"They were poachers. They should have been beaten and thrown in jail, not rewarded for their crimes."*

*"It was a man trying to provide for his children. These people barely manage to get by because of the taxes they pay to work the land. You should have seen this man and his family. They were skin and bones. I'd do it again if given the chance. It was the right thing to do and I don't care what our father does to me. There's nothing I could say to make this right in his eyes." Giovanni had found a poacher hunting on his father's estate. The protocol was to inform the guards and have the man arrested. But the man had begged and pleaded for mercy. He was only trying to feed his family after The Don had raised taxes. So instead of further adding to the man's hardship by informing his father, he started to sneak food out to the man. But his father had spies everywhere and he was soon found out.*

*His father was furious and had threatened to cane him until he was bloody. He was sent to the tower to reflect and pray over what he did. He was given a diet of bread and water while he remained in solitary confinement waiting for the brutal punishment to come. But it never did. It occurred to him that Adonis had spoken on his behalf. Adonis was the only one their father listened to, and many a time he'd spoken up on Giovanni's behalf.*

*"I admire your kind heart, brother, but there are certain things that just aren't done. You are the son of a* Duca. *You have to start acting like it."*

*"He doesn't treat me like I'm his son. I could be another servant for all he cares."*

*"Of course he cares."*

*"You keep saying that but we both know that isn't true. Adonis, I know you're just trying to protect my feelings but you don't have to lie."*

*Adonis sighed. "Well, I love you. You're my brother and I will always look out for you. One day I'll inherit the title and I'll need you to help me oversee the estate."*

*Besides Gio in the stables, Adonis was one of the few bright spots in his life. They were only two years apart but his older brother always looked out for him. There were times when Adonis could be a little arrogant in dealing with people he considered beneath him, but Giovanni put that down to his parents' influence. Adonis had a big heart and Giovanni loved him more than anyone else in the world. "If I'm still around. I'd like to see the world one day."*

*"You can see the world, as long as you come back to here. You belong by my side, little brother."*

*Giovanni returned to his position on the ground and they sat in silence. No words were exchanged between them for several moments, but none were needed. It was a companionable quiet that gave Giovanni a sense of peace he hadn't felt in a while. His brother had that effect on him. Finally, he turned to Adonis with a smile. "Thank you," he whispered.*

*Adonis raised a dark red brow. "For what?"*

*"For saving me from a lashing."*

*Adonis shrugged. "That's what brothers do. We look out for each other. No matter what. So I don't understand why you didn't save me."*

*Giovanni frowned. "Save you from what?"*

*Adonis turned to face him. His eyes which were usually golden in color were now blood red. He opened his mouth to reveal pointed teeth. "Why didn't you save me?"*

*Giovanni scooted away from Adonis in horror as the older boy's face continued to morph into something monstrous. "Adonis! What's wrong with you?"*

*"You didn't save me!" Adonis's hands were now claws. Suddenly he sprang on to Giovanni and wrapped those creature-like hands around Giovanni's throat. "You didn't*

31

*save me," he yelled again. He lowered his head with his mouth wide, and sharp teeth glistening as if he was ready to bite.*

*Giovanni screamed. "I'm sorry! I'm so sorry!"*

"John! Wake up!"

Someone shook him vigorously and all he could think about was getting away from the red-eyed monster. He pushed against his attacker with a hard shove only. There was a feminine cry before he heard a loud thud.

Giovanni bolted to a sitting position and opened his eyes. He fought to catch his breath. It was just a dream. But he'd felt someone grab him.

He looked around to see Sydney on the floor. She seemed to be a bit disoriented and confused.

"I'm so sorry, Miss Lewis." He pushed the covers off and slid out of bed to help her up. When he gripped her arm to lend her support, he didn't feel that big jolt he'd experienced with their initial touch, but there were currents between them all the same. She must have felt it too because she pulled away as soon as she was on her feet. "Thanks," she muttered. "Uh, are you okay? I heard you screaming from all the way downstairs."

"Yes, it was just a dream."

"A bad one from the sound of it. I was starting to get worried about you. I was tempted to call the doctor."

He scratched his head in confusion. "Because I was screaming?"

"No. Because you've been asleep for the past three days. I had to check on you a few times, to make sure you were still alive. If you didn't get up to go to the bathroom, I definitely would have called for help."

"Three days? Are you sure?"

"I'm very certain. Ida and I took turns checking on you. You weren't kidding when you said you were exhausted when you showed up."

He racked his hand through his hair. Giovanni doubted she would believe him if he told her he hadn't had actual sleep for the past few century. It was one of the side effects of the dark magic he'd dabbled in. "What time is it now?"

"It's almost six. Dinner will be ready in a half hour. Why don't you wash up and come and join us. I have three other boarders at the moment and Ida's grandson arrived this morning so we have a pretty full house for dinner tonight. Usually everyone does their own thing but tonight..." she broke off with a chuckle. "I'm sorry for rambling. I'm sure you probably want your privacy."

She slowly backed away but Giovanni reached out and took her hand. "No! I mean, you don't have to hurry off on my account. I don't mind the conversation. I appreciate you checking up on me." He couldn't help but be struck by her natural beauty. Something within him wanted to pull her closer so he could feel the softness of her body against his. Reluctantly he released her hand out of fear that he'd do just that.

"It's no problem, John. I should probably go help Ida with dinner. We're looking forward to you joining us tonight."

"Likewise."

This time when she turned to leave, he let her go although he didn't want to. As disturbing as his dream had been, his focus was on her. He'd made a promise to Nya that he'd keep an eye on Sydney. He wondered what his friend would think if she found out that he was having some very naughty thoughts involving her last living descendant.

## Chapter Four

The last time Sydney had heard anyone scream the way John had was the night she'd lost her parents. There was absolute horror in his voice as he yelled the words, *I'm sorry*. Thinking it was too intrusive a question to ask, she didn't inquire about to whom he was apologizing. The fear she'd heard in his cries had her heading to his room as quickly as she could.

When she'd touched him to shake him awake, Sydney could feel the cold film of sweat that covered him. Clearly he was in distress that made him shake beneath her touch. She didn't expect him to react so violently by pushing her to the ground but Sydney realized John hadn't meant any harm by it. What did give her pause, however, were the electric waves that seemed to course through her body when he'd helped her off the floor. It was that same spark she'd felt when she'd touched him during their first meeting. Sydney wasn't sure what to make of it but it was something she couldn't pursue. Her boarders were off limits. Most of them didn't stay longer than a few months and even if they stayed beyond that, their living situation would be awkward if things didn't work out. Sydney had learned that lesson the hard way.

After the accident that claimed her family, it had taken months of rehabilitation, counseling, and learning how to live independently with her disability. Dating had been the furthest thing from her mind. Once she'd felt like she'd gotten to a place where she was ready for a little masculine companionship, she was met with one disaster after another. There were a couple guys who she'd really been in to but each one of them had turned out to be huge disappointments.

Tyrell Jenkins was one of those men. He was a saxophonist who she'd met at a bar she played at on the weekends. He'd filled in for a sick member of a local band who also appeared at the same location. Sydney and Tyrell clicked right away and had a lot in common since they were both musicians. He was funny, charming and seemed to say all the right things. He was a gentleman who didn't act awkward around her because of her disability, not to mention, his deep sultry voice was enough to make her melt reminding Sydney of a smooth R&B singer. They dated casually for a few months when she started to believe that he might possibly be the one. He certainly had a way of making her feel special.

But then without a word, he abruptly left town with no explanation, leaving her to wonder what had gone wrong. She eventually got over him but it still hurt to know that she wasn't worth his effort to even explain why they didn't work out. It was as if he'd been toying with her all along.

Despite that setback with Tyrell, she'd kept herself open to romance which is how Dylan Beck happened. By the time Dylan had entered her life, Sydney had already established her independence and was running the boarding house successfully with Ida's help. Ida had mentioned her grandson was looking for a place to stay and asked if Sydney would be willing to set aside a room for Dylan whenever he was in town from one of his construction jobs. She'd been willing to pay to keep the room exclusively for Dylan. Of course, Sydney couldn't turn her friend down, after all Ida had done so much for her. So Dylan had become a semi-permanent resident at the house at no charge because Sydney refused to take money from Ida.

Sydney and Dylan had hit it off at first. He wasn't much of a talker but she enjoyed spending time with him. He seemed to say the right things and helped a lot around the house. Dylan encouraged Sydney in her musical pursuits and would listen to her play the piano for hours. He was always doing nice things for her like buying her favorite treat just because or going for long walks with her. Wherever she was so was he and Sydney soon became to depend on his presence. When he wasn't around she missed him. Though Sydney realized that it probably wasn't a good idea to get involved with Dylan because of the proximity of their living situation, she'd thrown caution to the wind and went on an official date with him when he'd asked.

Ida seemed to approve of the union as well, never missing a moment to say how good the couple looked together. Sydney didn't have to see with her eyes to know that Dylan was very attractive. He was tall and had a deep voice with a heavy southern lilt, which was basically the masculine version of his grandmother's. Dylan had long hair that she'd been told was jet black that fell to the center of his back, which he wore because of his heritage. He was half Catawba Indian, unlike his grandmother who was a full-blood. With his cheek bones, full lips and strong nose, he probably had no trouble attracting the opposite sex, so it was flattering that he was interested in her.

36

Things seemed to work out quite nicely for the two of them at first. Dylan was attentive and considerate. She enjoyed spending time with him, but then he became a different person. The change was gradual at first so Sydney shrugged it off when he started to make comments about her playing gigs. He wouldn't like it if she was out too late or who she was with, and sometimes he criticized her on how she dressed, saying she showed too much skin.

He'd once claimed to love her independence but slowly started to resent it. Dylan hated her friends and that she didn't want to spend every waking second with him. He began to question her whereabouts and who she spent time with. The final straw was when he came to the bar she worked at to start a fight with one of her friends who happened to belong to the house band. He claimed that the guy was hitting on her. It was clear to Sydney that Dylan saw her as a possession and not a person. Immediately after that incident she broke things off, fearful that his behavior would escalate if she remained in a relationship with him.

There had been an ugly blow-up when she'd told Dylan that she no longer wanted to date him. He'd yelled, cursed and shook her violently and for a moment she feared he might actually hurt her but he didn't. Instead, he disappeared for a few months much to her relief. It was only because he was Ida's grandson that she didn't kick him out of her house altogether. Of course Ida was disappointed that it didn't work out with Sydney and Dylan but thankfully the older woman didn't push the issue...at the time. But every now and then, Ida would make not-so-subtle hints about giving people second chances, which is exactly what she seemed to be doing now, and Sydney was very close to losing the last bit of patience she'd been holding on to since Dylan's return.

"Are you listening to me, Sydney?" Ida sounded more than a little irritated so Sydney could only imagine what her facial expression was.

"I'm sorry, Ida, my mind drifted for a moment."

"I was saying that I know things didn't work out with you and Dylan but I don't see any harm in the two of you being friends. You guys used to be so close."

Sydney had to bite her tongue to hold back the retort that nearly slipped. Sure she and Dylan had been close at one point but that was until he turned out to be a possessive psychopath. She sighed. "Ida, I know you wanted things to work out between me and your grandson but they just didn't. We can't go back to the way things used to be before we dated because they're just too awkward."

"I didn't say you had to be in a relationship with him again, just that you try to be friends with him. Whatever it was he did to make you angry with him, he's very sorry for. He's expressed his regret to me and he feels that you really haven't given him a chance to give you a proper apology."

Sydney could tell her friend had no intention of letting this go until she gave in. "Look, I'll talk to him, okay? But I can't make any promises beyond that. In the meantime, everyone is at the table ready for dinner. Could you please hand me a dish to put these mashed potatoes on?" She was sure to quickly change the subject to let Ida know that the subject was no longer up for discussion.

Ida patted Sydney's hand. "That's all I ask for."

They worked in silence putting the food in serving dishes. When Sydney would finish filling one bowl or plate, Ida would take it to the dining room. When she came back from delivering the last item, Ida smacked her lips. It was a sound Sydney knew too well. Ida was displeased.

Before Sydney could ask what the problem was, Ida volunteered. "I didn't expect to see that man at the table, especially after the way he was carrying on up there, screaming like the house was one fire."

"By that man, I assume you're referring to Mr. Chandler. I'm glad he could join us for dinner." She deliberately left out the conversation she'd had with him earlier and why he'd been screaming. It just seemed too personal to share, especially when Ida was already hostile toward the man.

"Well, I hope he fits in with everyone."

"I'm sure he will." Tired of this conversation, Sydney headed to the dining room and took her usual seat. The scent of Dylan's cologne alerted her to the fact that he took the seat next to her. Tempted to take another seat she thought better of it, not wanting to cause a scene.

"Sydney, you look lovely as usual," Dylan greeted.

"Thank you." Not wanting to entertain conversation with him she spoke to the rest of the diners. "Hope everyone enjoys dinner tonight. Smells like Ida made her famous meatloaf and I personally can't wait to dig in."

"Everything looks lovely, Sydney," Peter one of their on-again, off-again boarders replied. He was one of their older guests who lived up North but would come down to visit several weeks at a time to be close to his adult children and his grandkids. Not wanting to be a burden on his loved ones, he chose to stay at the boarding house when he visited. Sydney also suspected he continued to come because he had a thing for Ida, but her friend didn't seem to return his interest.

Two of her boarders were two college kids, Mikhail and Katrina from the Ukraine, who were in the United States for a summer work program. Their English wasn't very strong so they rarely participated in dinner conversation. Her last guest, Darlene Sullivan, preferred to take her meals in her room. She didn't socialize with the other guests, Ida or Sydney unless she was making demands. So it was surprising that she was at the table. Thankfully she sat on the opposite side of the table from Sydney which blunted the strong scent of a perfume that Darlene used way too liberally.

And then there was John Chandler.

Sydney could feel his gaze on her as she took her seat. Though she couldn't visually confirm it, she could feel it. She didn't understand why she suddenly felt self-conscious under his watchful stare.

As she fixed her plate, her usually dexterous grip became clumsy, causing her to nearly knock her glass over and fumble the serving dish. Dylan grabbed the tray from her and proceeded to finish the task for her. In most circumstances she would have been annoyed, but she couldn't shake that fluttering feeling she felt in the pit of her stomach as she wondered what John must have been thinking when he looked at her.

"You should be more careful, Sydney," Dylan interrupted her thoughts. "Lucky for you I'm here or there would be a big mess."

Sydney rolled her eyes. "Gee, I don't know how I got along without you all this time you've been away."

He leaned close enough for her to feel his breath against her ear. It took every ounce of willpower not to flinch away because Sydney was absolutely sure Ida was watching. "We need to talk," he whispered.

"We have nothing to talk about," Sydney spoke as softly as she could.

"You and I both know we have unfinished business."

"We've already gone over everything that needs to be said. Don't ruin this dinner for anyone else."

"I won't as long as you agree to meet me outside after dinner."

She took a deep breath. "Fine. Can I enjoy my dinner now?"

"By all means." She could hear the smug satisfaction in his voice and was actually glad she couldn't see the smirk that probably rested on his face; otherwise she'd be tempted to smack it off.

"So Miss Lewis, did you cook this delicious meal?" John Chandler's dulcet voice was a welcome distraction. She turned in the direction she'd heard him speak.

"No, you can thank Ida for the spread, although I did peel the potatoes. And please call me Sydney. We're not formal around here."

"And call me John."

A feeling of warmth spread throughout her body at the intimacy his tone took. She smiled. "Okay, John."

"I'm surprised you didn't have an accident handling a knife," Darlene piped up.

Sydney cringed on the inside at the sound of her demanding boarder's high-pitched voice. It was like nails raking down a chalkboard. "Why would you think there would be an accident?" She knew exactly what Darlene was trying to get at but she wanted to see if the other woman had the gall to come right out and say it. She'd bitten her tongue quite a bit whenever Darlene was around but she wasn't about to let the woman make her look incompetent, especially with a roomful of people. She might be blind but she was no pushover.

"Oh, I hope that didn't come out the wrong way. I just worry about you is all. I think it's amazing what you can do for someone with your…limitations."

Before Sydney could tell that bitch exactly where to go, Darlene started talking to John.

"So John, it's not often we get many handsome single men around here. What's your story?"

Now it made sense why Darlene had put in an appearance tonight. She must have caught sight of John. The woman was a barracuda.

"I don't really have much of a story to tell. I made a decent sum of money in the stock market in my twenties, got a bit burned out from the rat race and decided to cash in my earnings and see the world."

"Oh, that sounds exciting. I bet you've seen so much. I'd love it if you tell me about it sometime. Maybe you can to my room later for a drink and we can talk about it."

Sydney had been taking a bite of her meatloaf and nearly choked on it when she heard Darlene drop that tired line.

Dylan whacked Sydney's back. "Are you okay?"

Sydney broke into a fit of coughs. "I'm fine," she managed say before reaching for a glass of water.

"Sydney, sweetie, are you okay?" Darlene's fake concern made Sydney want to fling her mashed potatoes in that tramp's direction. The only thing that stopped her was not wanting to hit anyone else.

"I'm fine," she mumbled, embarrassed that she let the other woman get under her skin. She had no reason to be jealous, after all she barely knew John. And even if she broke her own rule about dating her boarders there was no guarantee that he had any interest in her beyond that of landlord and tenant.

The rest of the meal was an ordeal. Between Darlene's subtle barbs and Dylan finding any and all excuses to touch her, Sydney was ready to stab someone by the time she managed to get dinner down.

She excused herself before dessert to get some air and headed to the porch to clear her thoughts. When she heard footsteps shortly afterwards, she braced herself for another headache as she remembered she had promised Dylan a talk.

Without warning he placed his hands on her shoulders and pressed his lips to the back of her neck.

Sydney shoved her elbow into his midsection. "What the hell are you doing, Dylan? I didn't come out here for you to molest me." She turned toward him and made sure to put as much distance between them as possible.

"I've been gone for two months. I thought by now you would have gotten over it."

This asshole.

"Are you insane, Dylan? Get over it? You talk as if you didn't try to drive a guy's head through the wall. Stevie had a migraine for two weeks. You could have killed him and all because he was talking to me. That's not normal behavior. I'm lucky Dan even allows me to still play there."

"You didn't see how he was looking at you. That guy was undressing you with his eyes. No one is going to disrespect me or my girl like that."

"And that's what it all boils down to. Your ego was bruised and you had to display some brute force as a sign of your masculinity. Well, Dylan, I'm not your possession to fight over and to be perfectly honest, I'm not even interested in being your friend. As far as I'm concerned you're just a guest in my home and only because I care about your grandmother. Otherwise you could go straight to Hell."

"You're overreacting. You would have done the exact same thing in my position. Most women would be flattered that their men are looking out for them."

"Well, I'm not most women. And I wasn't flattered, as you put it. Flattering me would involve paying me a compliment. Telling me I looked beautiful or admiring my outfit, not nearly committing murder! Why you can't see what you did was wrong is beyond me. Not to mention you didn't even apologize. Don't you understand the enormity of what you've done? You're lucky Stevie or Dan didn't get the police involved. Just stay away from me, okay? And maybe you should look into shortening your visit this time around."

She attempted to move around him but he caught her by the wrist. "This isn't over," he growled. "You still belong to me and I'm not going to let you turn your back on me."

Sydney yanked her arm in an attempt to free herself but he tightened his grip. "Let me go!"

"You gave that new guy my room."

"Not that it's any of your business how I run my house, but your room was the only one that was ready when he arrived and I gave it to him because we didn't expect you for a few days. I don't even know why I'm even explaining this to you. Again I'd like to remind you that it's my house and I can do with it as I please. You're only in it as a courtesy to Ida. You don't even pay rent."

Before she was aware of what he was going to do she found herself locked in his arms. They were like bands squeezing her tight. When she would have screamed, Dylan covered her mouth in a bruising kiss.

"What's going on out here?"

Sydney nearly fainted in relief when she heard John's voice.

## Chapter Five

Giovanni wanted to leave the table as soon as he saw Dylan follow Sydney outside, but the redhead who'd taken a seat next to him at the dinner table clung to his arm like a second skin. Never one to mind the attention of beautiful women, he found Darlene annoying with her attempts to draw him into conversation. It didn't escape his notice that she took several subtle and not so subtle digs at Sydney. But he wasn't sure whether Sydney was more annoyed with the unwarranted shots Darlene sent her way or the presence of Dylan.

The other man switched between pawing Sydney and glaring at him, although it would have been quite obvious to anyone that Dylan's advances were unwelcome. He was surprised that the old woman Ida didn't seem to be bothered by Dylan's behavior; in fact, she pretended as if it wasn't happening. Even the two students who spoke Russian among themselves noted Sydney's discomfort. Only half-listening to them Giovanni understood what they were saying but gave nothing away. So when Sydney finally excused herself he thought that would be the end of it. But Dylan seemed to have other ideas. There was something about that guy Giovanni didn't like, even before he saw the way Dylan acted toward Sydney. Giovanni had a bad feeling about the guy but he couldn't quite put his finger on why.

It took some fancy maneuvering to work his way out of Darlene's grip but when he did, he headed to the door and could hear Sydney's raised voice. And then nothing. The sight that greeted Giovanni made him see red. Dylan's arms were wrapped tightly around Sydney as he pressed a desperate kiss against her lips. It was clear Sydney didn't enjoy Dylan's ardor. In fact she wiggled and squirmed in the other man's arms for dear life.

"Mind your business." Dylan grunted when Giovanni interrupted them while still keeping a tight grip on Sydney.

"It doesn't look like the lady returns your enthusiasm. I think you should let her go."

"Fuck off!" Dylan released Sydney so abruptly she stumbled backward but miraculously she managed to remain on her feet.

Seeing red, Giovanni advanced with fists clenched. Dylan, however, was ready for him because he swung his fist towards Giovanni's head. It looked like the other man was moving in slow motion because Giovanni was not only able to duck but he delivered a blow of his own, catching Dylan in the stomach.

Dylan crumpled to the ground, gasping for air.

Giovanni froze. Where did that come from? His reflexes had been lightning quick. That wasn't supposed to happen unless…was he getting his powers back? He didn't feel any differently, but he'd been able to perform that maneuver with the speed of an immortal.

He didn't have a chance to dwell on his abilities because he needed to make sure that Sydney was okay. Giovanni took her hand. "Are you all right?"

Sydney scrunched her nose in apparent confusion. "John? What happened?"

"Let's just say Dylan is down for the count."

"You knocked him out?"

"Um, he had the wind taken out of his sails but he's still cognizant from what I can tell."

"What's going on out here?" Ida appeared on the porch, looking none too pleased with the scene before her. When her dark gaze fell on the man still wheezing and rolling on the ground she hurried to his side. "Dylan!" She raised her head and glared at Giovanni. "What have you done to my grandson? Someone call the police." She yelled.

"No!" Sydney objected. "Dylan started it. John was defending me."

"Dylan isn't a troublemaker. We didn't have any problems before this one showed up." The old woman jerked her thumb in Giovanni's direction. A chill ran down his spine. If looks could kill, he'd be dead on the spot.

"Ida, why don't you help Dylan inside and we can talk about this later," Sydney interjected with diplomacy.

"You're taking his side? This man is a stranger. There's a rule against violence in this house and he violated it."

"Like I said, Dylan started it. Look, I know he's your grandson and you don't want to hear this but it's true."

Giovanni could tell Sydney's words weren't getting through to Ida. Even as she spoke, the old woman would not stop glaring at him.

Finally Dylan was able to sit up. He gasped for breath before speaking. "Leave it alone, Grandma. It's obvious Sydney doesn't understand the meaning of the word loyalty."

Sydney placed her hands on her hips. "Don't give me that, Dylan. You came out here with some bullshit and expect me to just be okay with it. Get over yourself. We're through."

Dylan laughed as he made it to his feet. "You keep telling yourself that and maybe you might even start believing it." He yanked himself away from his grandmother's grip before turning on Giovanni. "You got lucky, pretty boy. Next time you come at me, I'm going to knock your ass out." He then stormed into the house, leaving an open-mouthed Ida in his wake. Finally the old woman walked back inside, but not before shooting another glare in Giovanni's direction.

"Wow. That was intense." Sydney shook her head.

"I'll say."

And through it all, Giovanni still held her hand. Sydney must have noticed because she pulled her hand out his grip. "Sorry."

Giovanni wished he could take her in his arms just to feel her warmth against him. "Don't apologize. I didn't mind." He balled his fists at his sides to keep himself from cupping her face in his hands and kissing her pouty lips. She was so beautiful his heart sped up.

"To be honest, I don't want to go back inside and deal with the drama. Dylan is lurking in the house somewhere, Ida is probably pissed at me and I think if Darlene says anything else to me, I'm going to beat her with my cane."

Giovanni chuckled. "You don't seem prone to violence."

Sydney smiled. "You should have seen the fights I used to have with my sister. We'd go at it like a couple of wrestling pros."

"Then let's not go back in. Do you want to get out of here? Take a walk?"

She nodded. "Yeah, I think I'd like that."

He noticed that she didn't have her cane with her. "Do you need your cane?"

"I can get around the house pretty well without it, but I need it once I step outside, but like I said before I'd rather not go back inside right now. At least not until things cool down a little. So, if you don't mind guiding me, I don't need it."

His body quickened at the thought of her holding on to him. It might not have been a good idea, but he couldn't pass up the opportunity. "Of course not. Should I take you hand?"

"Just hold out your arm."

Giovanni followed her instruction and she wrapped her arms around his bicep. Her touch was like a balm to his soul. Giovanni willed his fast hardening cock to stay at rest.

Sydney must have sensed his discomfort. "Are you okay?"

"Yeah, I uh, I'm just admiring the view."

She smiled, released small even white teeth. "That's one thing about being blind that I miss out on, the stars. I used to sit in my parents' back yard at night with a blanket and stare at them for hours. Are there a lot out tonight?"

Though the view he referred to was her beauty, he didn't want to make her uncomfortable. "Yes. The sky is littered with them." He didn't know if that was true or not because he couldn't take his gaze off her.

"Sounds lovely."

"Very lovely. Let's go."

They walked in silence for a while. Sydney knew the exact moment when they stepped off her property because she counted the steps. She wasn't sure what it was about this stranger that made her feel so comfortable and safe but being besides him just felt right. She was playing with fire by being out here with him. Sydney promised herself that after tonight she would keep a friendly distance between herself and John but for now, she wanted to enjoy being in his presence.

"I don't think anyone has stood up to Dylan like that. He can be a bit of a hothead."

"I didn't like the way he grabbed you. Has he been rough like that with you before?"

"When we were together no, but when we broke up, he didn't take it too well. He didn't hit me but I feared that he would. He shook me until my teeth rattled. I'm just lucky he didn't take things further"

"If you don't mind me asking, what made you break up with him?"

"Besides his temper? He was jealous and wanted to know where I was every second of the day. I couldn't deal with it. I guess he thought because I'm blind, he could control me and I'd be grateful that someone was willing to date me, but that shit gets old real quick."

"I can't say I blame you. It must be awkward living with him in the same house."

Sydney laughed without humor "Tell me about it. Fortunately his work takes him away often so I don't have to deal with him that much. So, tell me about you, John Chandler. You mentioned earlier about traveling. That must be pretty exciting. Where are some of the places you've visited?"

"I've seen most of the world. I have more stamps in my passport than the post office."

She giggled. "Really? Have you been to Paris?"

"Several times."

"Is it as beautiful as I imagine it to be?"

"Depends on what you consider beautiful. Paris is old, as are a lot of its buildings. So if your thing is history, then Paris is the place for you. Although, I must admit that there's nothing as breathtaking as the Paris skyline at night."

"That sounds incredible. I've always wanted to go there but I haven't had the chance. I might not be able to see the sights but I just want to be there to hear the sounds and experience the smells, taste the food."

"Why haven't you traveled?"

She shrugged. "It's always something. I lost my family and my sight in a really bad car accident. I was nineteen at the time and I had so many plans. I wanted to somehow make a living playing music. The future was mine. And then in a blink of an eye my world was shattered. I understandably went through a lot of counseling and rehabilitation. By the time I felt like I could live life again, I realized I didn't want to live in my parents' house without them, so I sold it and with the money from that sale combined with the settlement from the insurance company I bought the old boarding house. It was a major fixer upper but I didn't mind. I hired some contractors to get it up to code. But since it's an old house it requires a lot of love. One year the furnace stopped working, and another time I needed to replace the hot water heater, and once we got hit hard by a hurricane."

"Sounds like a money pit."

Sydney knew it must seem like a burden to someone else but she adored this house. When she and her sister were kids, they used to ride their bikes down the dirt path to this abandoned house. While Tara thought the house was icky and haunted as most of the local children did, Sydney had seen the character in the old structure. She imagined what it would look like in its glory.

Granted she couldn't see all the work that had been put in to it, but she knew it was beautiful.

"It's a treasure. It's my dream house. I loved it when I saw it as a kid and love it even more as an adult. I know this sounds silly, but sometimes I like to walk against the walls just to run my fingers along the crown molding. I also like that my house has a story to tell. It was built shortly after the Civil War by a wealthy family from the North. The locals didn't take too kindly to these carpetbaggers coming to their town and flaunting their wealth, particularly when everyone around them were still suffering from the devastation of war. So the townspeople ran them out. Shortly afterward, the house was bought by a Scottish man who turned it into a house of ill repute."

"Is that so?"

"Yes, it was a part of a major scandal. Around the fifties the mayor was caught in the house with his mistress. Shortly afterwards the operation was shut down."

"That's quite a story."

"It is. You can't find that with all these modern monstrosities that they build now. They have no soul." She laughed. "I'm sorry. I'm probably boring you."

"Not at all. I find this fascinating. You mentioned that you wanted to play music for a living at one point. I notice a piano in the sitting room. Do you play?

"Yes. I usually play when one of the residents requests it but for the most part I play keyboards at a bar a couple weekends a month. It doesn't pay much but I do it because I love it."

"I'd love to hear you play sometimes."

"You're on. I love the classics but my favorite is jazz and modern. I have to admit that when I start playing I can get carried away. I don't just play the piano though. I'm proficient with the guitar and clarinet as well. " She broke off with a laugh. "Once again I feel like I'm talking too much."

"I don't mind."

"Even still, I've dominated the conversation. Why don't you tell me more about you? What does your family think of you traveling so much?"

She felt him stiffen beneath her touch and Sydney wondered if she'd touched a nerve. "You don't have to talk about it if you don't want to. I'm being too intrusive."

"No, it isn't that. I'm not exactly sure how to explain it. My father died a long time ago and my mother recently passed. I wasn't particularly close with her."

"But you were with you father?"

"Very much so."

"Were you an only child?"

No, I have brothers. I recently lost my oldest brother and I'm not very close with my four younger ones but I wish I was."

"I'm sorry for your loss."

"It's okay. It was inevitable."

That was an odd way of putting it. "Was he sick?"

"You could say that."

The fact that he didn't elaborate, indicated to her she shouldn't push the issue, but he did mention other siblings. "Why aren't you close to your other brothers?"

"It's complicated."

There was pain in his words, and though Sydney wanted to know more, she didn't dare ask because she didn't want to end this feeling she had while she was with him. "I'm sorry" Sydney wasn't sure what she was apologizing for, maybe all of it but she felt that John had suffered through a lot.

"Thank you."

They continued to walk in silence until a cool breeze caressed her face. She halted. "Mmm, do you feel that?" She lifted her face to the sky.

"The wind?"

"Yes. After this oppressive heat it feels so good."

John didn't respond.

Wanting to hear his voice again, she asked, "What's the favorite place you've visited?"

"Honestly?"

"Yeah."

"Here."

She raised a brow as she faced him. "Really? You've been all over the world and this hole-in-the-wall town is what you pick? Why?"

"Because you're here."

Before Sydney could process what he'd said, his lips were on hers. And unlike the kiss she'd experienced earlier, this one was welcome.

## Chapter Six

Giovanni couldn't help himself. Walking next to Sydney with her body practically pressed against his was absolute torture. She smelled of honey and lavender. The softness of her skin beneath his fingertips drove him crazy. The longer he stayed in her presence he could feel a change take place within him. His eyesight seemed to sharpen and everything seemed louder. It was difficult to keep his heart rate under control. It was beating erratically. And when Sydney turned her beautiful face in his direction, he couldn't help himself. He just needed a taste of those lips that had been tempting him all night. He figured if he could sample her lips just once, she could cease being an obsession to him.

He cupped her face in his hands and moved his mouth over hers, reveling in the softness of her mouth beneath his. He'd been fighting a hard on all night from just being near her, and now his cock was so stiff he could barely contain himself. He pressed his erection against the juncture of her thighs.

Sydney moaned softly against his mouth parting her lips to grant him access, but Giovanni took his time savoring her. He ran his tongue along the seam of her lips, tasting the spices from their dinner, and something fruity. She tasted of pure heaven.

Sydney threaded her fingers through his hair and pressed her tongue forward to meet his. She swirled her tongue around his, actively participating in the kiss which only served to turn him on even more.

He slid his hands down the length of her body, committing them to memory. Giovanni continued his exploration until he grabbed her plump rear which he used as leverage to pull her even closer. He grinded against her unable to get enough of Sydney.

What he wanted most was to throw her on the ground, explore every inch of her body and fuck her senseless. He broke the kiss long enough to whisper against her lips, "You're so fucking beautiful. I've thought of nothing but this since I laid eyes on you." Instead of returning to her mouth he pressed his lips against her pulse before licking her skin. He sucked her flesh into his mouth aggressively knowing that there would be a mark later but in that moment he didn't care. He wanted to claim her, make her his.

"Ouch!" Sydney cried out.

Hearing the pain in her voice he immediately released her.

"Y-you bit me." Sydney's hand flew to the spot where he'd nipped her.

"I'm sorry. I got a bit carried away."

Sydney furrowed her brow. "You sound funny. Are you okay?"

It wasn't possible. Giovanni touched his teeth. His incisors had lowered. This. Wasn't. Supposed. To. Happen. He was mortal wasn't he? He willed them to retract as he'd done thousands of times before but they wouldn't go away.

He took a step away from her.

"John?" Sydney pressed.

"I'm fine. I think we should head back. I'm sorry for crossing the line. That won't happen again."

"The kiss or you biting me?"

"Both. Just give me a minute, okay? I need to catch my breath." Giovanni took another few steps away from her. Once his got his breathing under control he felt his incisors retreat. Giovanni realized then that somehow Sydney was affecting his body in ways he didn't expect she would. It brought to mind what had happened on the porch with Dylan. His speed had been unlike anything it had been since he'd undergone the purge and when he'd hit Dylan, Giovanni didn't think he used enough force to take down such a solid man but Dylan had crumpled like a folding chair. Something was happening to him that he didn't quite understand, and Sydney was the key.

He needed to get in contact with Steel right away to find out what was going on with him but in the meantime, he had to take the long, torturous walk back to Sydney's house. He hoped he'd be able to make it back without doing something stupid.

Giovanni moved next to her. "Here, take my arm."

This time when she gripped him it wasn't as tightly as she had when they'd began their walk. "Before you say it John, I will. I really enjoyed that kiss more than anything I have in a long time. But it was a mistake."

That's exactly what he was going to tell her but hearing it from her lips was like a knife to the heart. Giovanni didn't reply, not trusting himself to speak.

"I mean, you're a boarder in my home and I've made it a rule not to date one. I've already made that mistake with Dylan and as you see, that didn't turn out too well. You seem like a nice guy, but this was a one-time thing, okay?"

"I agree." It actually caused him physical pain to get those words out but it was for the best. If he was turning back into a vampire, he wasn't sure if the purge had actually worked. He feared that all the black magic he used to practice would return tenfold and put Sydney in danger. Until he figured out his next course of action, he'd have to stay clear of her, even if the prospect of that was pure torture.

Dante Grimaldi paced his living room floor, unable to shake the uneasy feeling he had. He'd felt it for the past couple days and couldn't figure out why. He'd checked on his brothers to assure himself that everything was okay with them. GianMarco and Maggie were doing well, so well in fact they were expecting another child. Vampires weren't the most fertile of creatures, so he was surprised that they were expecting so soon after having a child not too long ago, but he was happy for them. Those two had been through so much. They deserved every bit of happiness that came their way.

Niccolo and Sasha were busy helping their son plan his nuptials to his mate Camryn. Romeo and Christine were enjoying their children. For once there was no danger or turmoil in his life and while Dante was happy about that, he couldn't figure out why this unsettling sensation had taken hold of him.

"If you keep pacing like that, you're going to wear a hole in the carpet." Isis walked behind him and wrapped her arms around his waist. He loved this woman with every breath in his body. He shuddered when he thought about how he nearly destroyed his chances at love and all because of his stubborn pride.

"I'm sorry, *bellissima*. I have a lot on my mind."

"Like what?"

Dante gently removed her arms from around him so he could turn to face her. "It's probably nothing, but I have a premonition that something is wrong and it feels like it has something to do with one of my brothers, but I've contacted them all and everything is fine with them. Better than fine actually."

Isis stroked his face and placed a light kiss on Dante's lips. "Maybe part of the problem is the fact that you can't relax. You've spent the majority of your life focused on taking down *Il Diavolo*. And now he's no longer a threat you don't know what to do with yourself. Sure there will always be rouges and problems and evil that The Underground will have to deal with, but nothing on the magnitude of what we recently faced. Maybe one day there will be another villain of that caliber but for now there isn't. Stop looking for trouble when there is none."

A smile tilted his lips. She was probably right except his sixth sense when it came to his family had never let him down before. "I wish I had your confidence, but something just doesn't sit well with me."

Isis ran her palm down the center of his body stopping just above his cock. He groaned. "Are you trying to distract me, woman?"

She grinned. "Is it working?"

He pulled her into his arms and buried his face against her neck, inhaling her magnificent scent. Just as he was about to carry her to their bedroom where he could make love to her properly, an image of red eyes flashed in his mind. That feeling he'd experienced hit him harder than ever. He pulled away from his bloodmate.

She furrowed her brows in concern. "What is it?"

"Something is definitely wrong." Dante raked his fingers through his hair

"But you said yourself that your brothers are fine unless...."

"Unless what?"

"What about Giovanni? He is your brother too."

"Shit," he muttered. "That must be it. He'd built such a strong barrier around himself over the years that I never felt the connection to him except when he wanted to let me in. Other than that, I could never feel him. If it is indeed what I feel right now, he's in trouble of some sort. But I have no way of getting in contact with him."

"You could always have some of your agents go on a lookout for him."

"Yes, but he's my brother, and this is probably something I should do myself. I'll talk to Marco, Ro and Nico to see what they have to say about it."

Isis sighed. "Looks like you're gearing yourself up for another mission."

"I wouldn't call it that exactly, it's more of a family matter. Giovanni took Adonis's death hard. And while I can't say I'm sorry Adonis is gone, he was our brother as well. Giovanni knew him before he did all those horrible things, so it's understandable that he'd mourn that loss more than the rest of us. The last time I spoke to him, his pain was deep, he was hurting and there was no way I could convince him that it wasn't his fault that Adonis died. It was either us or him."

"Maybe he needs to realize that Adonis died long before his body actually did. He wasn't the same person."

"I thought about that but with the events being so recent, I doubt Giovanni feels the same. But now he's in some sort of trouble and I'll be damned if I let him suffer on his own."

"Then let me help. Wherever you go, I go."

Dante released a deep breath and pressed his forehead against his bloodmate's. He didn't know how he'd gotten by without her for so long. "Thank you," he whispered.

"For what?"

"For being you. I love you."

"I love you too, Dante. Whatever Giovanni is going through right now we'll help him with it. We all will."

"But first we have to find him."

Dylan stood on the porch waiting for Sydney's return. With each passing second he grew angrier thinking about how that bastard was touching her. If he hadn't been sucker punched, Dylan would have fucked that guy up. He wasn't sure if he was more upset at the outsider for interfering in something that didn't concern him or at Sydney for going off with that motherfucker. Where was her loyalty? According to his grandmother, John Chandler had only been in residence for a few days and most of that time he'd spent sleeping. Sydney needed to learn that she belonged to him. That other guy was only toying with her emotions just to see what it would be like with a blind chick. He on the other hand actually cared about her, after all, who else would want a woman who couldn't see? She should be grateful that he wanted her and when he got the chance to talk to her again, he'd let her know exactly that. First he would wait for her to get back and then he'd send John Chandler packing.

John Chandler. Something about that guy didn't seem right. It didn't slip Dylan's attention that whenever a question was asked of him at dinner he never gave a direct answer. What was he hiding? Whatever it was,

Dylan intended to find out and get that bastard out of here.

"What are you doing out here?" His grandmother stepped onto the porch, her arms crossed.

"Waiting for Sydney. She's been gone with that guy for a while."

"Don't go causing any more trouble, Dylan. You've done enough damage tonight." She shook her head at him. The way his grandmother stared at him spoke of her disappointment, though she'd never come right out and say it.

"I didn't start it. He shouldn't have gotten involved in something that wasn't any of his business. If you'll remember he was the one who attacked me."

"As much as I love you Dylan, I also know you're not completely innocent. You have your mother's temper. I couldn't tell her a thing either. When she wanted something she went after it. That's how she ended up with that no-account father of yours. I told her that man was trouble but she wouldn't listen. Said he would take her away to the big city and give her the life she deserved." She sucked her teeth like she did when she was annoyed.

His grandmother basically raised him since he was ten because his mother never stuck around longer than the time it took her to find another man to have some fun with. Dylan had only met his father once. He was an executive for a big food company that required him to be travel a lot, which was how he met Dylan's mother. While his mother Maureen saw him as her meal ticket, he saw her as a fling. Kevin Peterson was already married with three children, and he had no intention of leaving his perfect white family for a dirt poor Indian whore and her half-breed offspring. At least that's the way his grandmother liked to tell the story.

When Dylan was fourteen, he was determined to meet the man neither his mother nor grandmother talked much about. He'd found his father's address among some letters his mother had kept and Dylan had stolen some money from his grandmother's rainy day fund that she kept under her bed and took a bus to the address. To say his meeting with Kevin had been disappointing would have been putting it lightly. Not only did he pretend not to know who Dylan was despite the strong resemblance, he'd threatened to call the police. Dylan had caught sight of one of his siblings, a boy not much older than him who looked at him with contempt. Dylan had left after that but he vowed that one day he'd get even.

"You never miss an opportunity to remind me, do you?"

"I mention it because you keep screwing up. That temper of yours is going to get the better of you one day. You've already been to jail for more times than I can count. The sheriff has a permanent cot set up for you. The next time the judge might not be so lenient."

"That won't happen as long as —"

Ida glared. "Shut up. I told you not to speak of that. Maybe you should give Sydney some space. She could still come around."

Maybe, but as long as that John Chandler is around, I can't make any promises."

"You let me take care of that."

"What do you plan on doing?"

"Don't worry about it. Just give it a few days and I guarantee, Sydney will see things differently very soon."

Dylan narrowed his eyes, wondering what his grandmother was up to. She could be very persuasive when she wanted to be, and he didn't know what she had planned. But then he thought about his woman doing God-knows-what with that outsider and it made his blood boil. He wouldn't ask questions for now. As long as it resulted in Sydney being his again.

## Chapter Seven

*Giovanni brushed his horse with vigorous strokes, preparing it for his daily ride as Gio and he casually chatted. They could speak more freely now that Gio had been promoted to stable master after the death of the previous one. "You seem a little quieter than usual," Gio observed.*

*Giovanni shrugged. "I'm not sure why it is, but something doesn't feel right. I can't help but think something is going to happen soon. Something bad."*

*Gio closed the distance between the two of them and placed his hands on Giovanni's shoulders. "What's going on? Remember, you can tell me anything."*

*And Giovanni knew that to be true. Besides Adonis, there was no one he felt more comfortable with than Gio. It was why he spent so much time in the stables. "My father's family is visiting and they don't like me or Adonis. I hear them whisper, saying me and Adonis look nothing like our father. Mama says they're just trying to cause trouble."*

*When Gio didn't say anything, Giovanni glanced up to catch his reaction. His friend had gone pale as if he'd seen a ghost.*

*"Gio? Are you all right?"*

*The stable master slowly nodded. "Yes. Well, like your mother said, they're just trying to cause trouble, I'm sure." He turned his back abruptly and Giovanni had the distinct impression that his friend was hiding something.*

*He didn't get a chance to pursue the topic because he heard the sound of footsteps drawing near. "Giovanni!"*

*It was Adonis.*

*"I'm here," he called out to his brother.*

*Adonis rounded the corner. His face was nearly as red as his hair. He looked agitated. "I should have known you were out here. Why are you grooming your horse? That's the stable boy's job."*

*Giovanni shrugged. "I like doing it. What's wrong with you?"*

*"Our cousins are making trouble again. I needed to get out of the castle. Are you about to go for a ride? If you are I'd like to join you."*

*"Yes, I am."*

*"Good." Adonis snapped his finger and one of the stable boys came running to do his bidding. "Prepare my horse and be quick about it."*

*Adonis must have really been in a mood. Even though he could be quite arrogant toward the servants when he wanted to be, he wasn't usually this rude. Giovanni noticed that Gio made himself scarce to give them some privacy.*

*Once the horses were ready and they were a safe distance away from the stables, Giovanni broke the silence that had fallen between them. "Tell me, what's happened to upset you."*

*"Papa and I were in his study. He wanted to show me the bookkeeping so I would know the extent of our wealth when I inherit everything from him. Cousin Fabricio was also there. He began to make comments about me not looking anything like our father. He kept bringing up my red hair and said no male in the Sarducci family has ever had my hair color. But our mother has red hair. Papa said the same thing and cousin Fabricio seemed to agree but he kept hinting that I wasn't a real Sarducci. Papa told him to be quiet and he would for a while but he'd start up again. I was so angry, I hit him."*

*Giovanni raised a brow. It wasn't like his brother to lose his cool in front of their father or at all for that matter. "What did our father say?"*

*"I didn't give him a chance to say anything. I ran out the castle and went looking for you."*

*"You shouldn't listen to them. They are troublemakers. They come here twice a year, eat a lot, gossip and cause trouble. No one takes them seriously."* Giovanni hoped his response was enough to calm his brother down, although at least he actually looked like one of their parents. Giovanni, on the other hand, looked like neither. He'd heard the servants gossip about his paternity when they didn't think anyone was listening. It often made him wonder about the validity of those claims. At least then it would make sense why his father treated him the way he did. But he recognized that hearing something like that would be devastating for his brother, who was the favored son.

*"You're right. What does Fabricio know anyway? He's jealous because he won't inherit all this and I will."*

Giovanni nodded. *"That's exactly it. Jealousy."*

Adonis smiled. *"Thank you, Giovanni."*

*"For what?"*

*"You always manage to make me feel better. How about we race to the end of the field?"*

Before Giovanni could agree, his brother took off. He smacked his horse's rear to take it from a gallop to a run in order to catch up to his brother. Adonis might have been older, but Giovanni was the better rider, mainly because of all the time he spent in the stables.

Giovanni caught up to Adonis and beat him by a nose.

Adonis didn't seem bothered by his defeat. *"I almost had you that time."*

*"Almost, but not quite."*

*"Giovanni?"*

*"Yes, Adonis?"*

*"Can I ask you a question?"*

*"What is it?"*

*"Why didn't you save me?"*

*Giovanni turned his head to ask Adonis what he was talking about. To his shock and horror, his brother, who still sat astride his horse, had a trail of blood trickling down both sides of his mouth. There was a huge fist-sized hole in the middle of his chest.*

*"Why didn't you save me?" Adonis asked again before his eyes turned bright red.*

Giovanni sat up in his bed with a start. The dream had seemed so real. It was a cross between an actual memory and a nightmare, just like before. He remembered that day when Adonis had come looking for them when Fabricio had upset him. And then they raced their horses. That had happened shortly before their mother was found to be having an affair with Gio. It was revealed that the man who Giovanni had seen as a father figure was actually their real father.

It was getting to a point where he didn't want to go to sleep because he'd be reminded of a past that still haunted him and probably would continue to for the rest of his life.

A soft knock on the door interrupted his thoughts. "Who is it?"

"It's Sydney. Are you okay in there?"

Sydney.

After their kiss Giovanni had spent the next couple of days avoiding her, only joining the house for meals. During the day, he went for long walks to clear his head. The local library had also been a welcome distraction that kept him occupied and away from the house. Sydney seemed to be doing the same so he was surprised that she'd be outside his room.

He slid out of bed and grabbed his pajama pants and quickly slid into them. It didn't matter that she couldn't see his nudity; Giovanni needed that barrier between them in case he did something stupid. Whenever he was around her, he couldn't think straight.

He opened the door just enough to see her face. Giovanni barely managed not to gasp. Once again he was struck by her beauty. Even without a drop of makeup her skin glowed and he wanted nothing more than to have another taste of her sweet lips. Wrapped in a fluffy pink terry robe, Sydney caused Giovanni to imagine what her body looked like beneath it. And beneath him. He needed to get her away from him quickly before he did something stupid. "Yes, everything is okay. Was there anything you wanted?"

She nibbled her bottom lip seeming slightly hesitant. "I was on my way to my room when I heard you cry out. Did you have another nightmare?"

"I'm sorry if I was loud. I'll try to keep it down."

"The noise isn't a problem. It wasn't the blood-curdling scream like the first time, but I noticed the last couple nights, you seemed to wake up yelling. I know it's none of my business, but are you sure everything is okay?"

Giovanni pinched the bridge of his nose to compose himself. He knew she was just being nice but he didn't think he could handle her kindness... not now, not when he didn't feel like he deserved it. "You're right Sydney. It's none of your business." The moment he said it, he wanted to cut his own tongue out because her face completely crumbled. He'd hurt her and it was like a kick in his own gut.

She backed away. "Well, I'm sorry to bother you then. Have a good night."

When she would have turned away, he grabbed her by the wrist. "I'm sorry. I shouldn't have said that. I'm just a little irritable is all. Please come in."

Sydney stiffened. "I'm not sure if that's a good idea."

"Please. I promise I won't try anything."

"I wasn't worried about that," she said a little too quickly.

"Then come in. I could use the company. It's not like I'm in a hurry to get back to sleep." Against his better judgment he moved aside so that she could step inside, which she did.

Giovanni took a quick peek down the hall to make sure no one else lingered around. He then closed the door behind her so they could talk in private. Walking over to the desk in the corner of his room, he pulled out the chair for her. "Have a seat. The chair directly behind you."

She turned to feel for it before sitting down. "Thank you."

Giovanni sat on his bed across the room to place as much distance as he could between the two of them. "Again, I apologize for any disturbance I caused. Shortly before I came here, I had what one would probably call an extreme sense of insomnia. A lot of nights I would have loved to sleep. And now, I dread it."

"Because of the nightmares?"

The compassion etched on Sydney's lovely face made him feel a little ashamed for entertaining these carnal thoughts of her. Even now as he watched her across the room, his cock stirred. He'd never been more aware of a woman in his life. He'd had lovers over the course of his life and he'd enjoyed many of them, but none of them made him feel so alive and aware of his body's needs.

He nodded and then remembered she couldn't see that gesture. "Yes. Every night when I fall asleep I dream about things that will probably haunt me for the rest of my life."

71

"I'm sorry to hear that, John. I kind of know how you feel."

Giovanni laughed without humor. "You couldn't possibly know what this feels like. I lost someone close to me and I did everything in my power to save him but apparently it wasn't enough and I have to live with the "what ifs" for the rest of my life. I have to wonder what I could have done differently, and if I'd chosen a different path maybe things wouldn't have turned out the way they did." He wasn't sure why he'd told her that. Giovanni hadn't told anyone about the guilt he felt over Adonis's death, not Nya, or his other brothers. He knew Nya carried her own guilt where Adonis was concerned, and as for the other four, they wouldn't understand. They hated Adonis and justifiably so, but he'd be damned if he allowed them to tarnish the memory of the brother he'd once known. Somehow, telling Sydney just felt right and he was compelled to tell her more.

"And what kills me is that no one else knows the real him. They will never understand what he went through and what was done to make him the way he was. My brother was my best friend and I fought so hard for him even when he stopped fighting for himself. And these nightmares are my punishment for not saving him." Tears stung the backs of his eyes but he refused to let them fall. He couldn't. He didn't deserve to unburden himself of the pain. There would be no atonement for him.

Giovanni gripped his hands in his lap so hard he felt as if his bones would break. He sat very still for several long moments in an attempt to get his emotions under control. When he was certain he wouldn't have a breakdown, he noticed Sydney hadn't said anything.

He looked up to see tears spilling unheeded down her cheeks.

Giovanni sprang to his feet and was at her side in an instant. He knelt down and took her hand. "I'm sorry. I didn't mean to upset you."

She quickly swiped her tears away with the back of her free hand and then shook her head. "No. You didn't. I just feel terrible that you're going through this. Your brother must have been very special."

"He was."

"Then I don't think he'd want you to hurt this way. I'm sure there's a lot you're not telling me and that's okay. It's your story to tell, but do you honestly believe your brother would want you to hold on to this guilt?"

"Probably not, but it's really not that simple. You wouldn't understand."

"You keep saying that as if I've never experienced loss. I deal with loss every single day of my life. How do you think it feels when I wake up in the morning and I hear the sound of a bird chirping and I'm not able to look out the window and see it flying around? When I'm out in public and I hear a baby cry and I can't see its face? Memories that used to be so keen in my mind are becoming faded and distant. Besides that, I feel guilt too. My parents and my sister were taken away by a bunch of drunk teenagers going on a joy ride. Even though I lost my sight, I ask myself everyday 'why me?' Why did I survive and they didn't? There are days when I think it would have been better if I'd gone too because then I wouldn't have to live with the pain of missing them so much. I'll never be able to give my mother a hug or listen to one of my father's corny jokes. I won't get to see my best friend again. My little sister was only seventeen so why them and not me? You don't have the market on guilt. And trust me, my nightmares are just as real as yours."

Her words were like a kick in his gut. Giovanni felt like an asshole for not considering her ordeal. He already knew about her accident and family history because of what Nya had told him and his own research he'd done on her. "My apologies for being so self-absorbed."

"There's no need to feel bad. I only mentioned it to say, I can imagine how you feel. I might not be able to fully understand because our experiences are our own, but I do empathize." She reached out and touched his face and immediately yanked her hand away. She shifted in her chair and let out an uneasy giggle. "I'm sorry. I have a habit of being very touchy-feely. It may seem cliché but it's kind of my way of seeing how people look."

Giovanni took her hand and placed it against his cheek. "I don't mind. Look all you'd like."

Sydney seemed hesitant.

"Go ahead," he insisted.

Slowly she brought her other hand up and stroked the sides of his face. Sydney grazed her thumbs along the ridge of his brow before gently caressing his hair. "What color is your hair?"

"Black."

"And your eyes?"

His breath caught in his throat making it nearly impossible for him to get the words out but somehow he managed. Sydney had no idea what she was doing to him. "Green."

"That sounds like a nice combination." She skimmed his nose with the tips of her fingers.

When she touched his lips, Giovanni moaned, unable to help himself. He was so fucking hard, he couldn't think straight. He wasn't sure how he would be able to contain himself if she continued. It was on the tip of his tongue to tell her it might be a good idea if she left but something unexpected happened.

Sydney leaned forward and pressed her lips against his.

## Chapter Eight

When Sydney heard John crying out as she walked to her room, her first instinct was to mind her own business and keep going. The situation between them was already tense and awkward, with each of them going out of their way to avoid the other. But she'd found herself knocking on his door because she couldn't turn her back on his pain. It just wasn't in her.

She even knew it was a bad idea to be alone with him in his room but she couldn't turn his offer down. Though she couldn't explain it, there seemed to be some kind of force that drew her to this mysterious man. It made her want to know more about him. It had broken her heart to hear how he tortured himself over the loss of his brother.

Once she had been assured that he was okay, she should have left, but unable to leave well enough alone she found herself touching him. His face was strong and she imagined him to be quite handsome. It certainly made sense now why Darlene had fawned all over him. Unable to help herself she pressed her lips against his. She told herself that it was his heady scent, the way his breath hitched in his throat or maybe it was the way his heart throbbed beneath his touch. Whatever the reason she kissed him, the moment she felt his sensual lips beneath hers, her body instantly went up in flames. In a brief moment of clarity it dawned on Sydney how precarious her situation was and she attempted to pull away, but John pulled her closer.

He cupped the back of her head, taking complete control of the kiss. He pressed his tongue past her slightly parted lips and swirled it around as if he wanted to explore every nook and cranny of his mouth. He tasted amazing. It was like chocolate, mint, and something tangy and bold like a fine wine. Sydney grasped his shoulders and pushed her tongue forward to meet his, wanting to savor ever moment. She'd experienced many kisses before but none that made her toes curl and ignite her senses. Sydney believed she could get drunk from his kisses. The head rush made her head spin but in a good way.

With a growl, John yanked her out of her chair and lifted her into his arms. Instinctively, Sydney wrapped her arms around his neck and her legs around his waist as she felt the sensation of being carried. It felt like she was floating. His arms were strong like corded ropes and she'd never felt more secure than she did in this moment. "So beautiful," he muttered against her mouth before tugging her bottom lip between his teeth. She dug her fingers through his silky locks. Her pussy throbbed, and the need to be closer to him was all she could think about. Sydney's nipples pressed painfully against her pajama top.

She grinded against him to temper the ache within her core.

Gently, he placed her on the bed and opened her robe. He slid into the bed next to her and ran kisses over her face and neck as he unbuttoned her top. With each button he opened, he'd place a kiss on the skin he exposed, all while avoiding her breasts. She squirmed wanting to feel his mouth all over her. Sydney wanted desperately to 'see' him. He was bare-chested which made it easy for her to freely explore his body. She could feel his well-developed torso and the defined muscles. She moaned when her fingers encountered rippled abs.

"You're beautiful," she murmured.

"You seem so sure of it." She could hear the smile in his voice.

"Oh, I can tell. I may not be able to see with my eyes, but other senses haven't let me down." She ran a finger over his peck and found nipple. It fascinated her how it puckered beneath her fingertip.

John inhaled sharply.

Sydney leaned forward to press a kiss against his chest and followed it with a swipe of her tongue. The salty taste of his skin and musk made an intoxicating cocktail.

He chuckled as he pushed her down. "Patience, *gattina*. You have no idea how long I've wanted this. I want to take my time with this beautiful body."

She found it an odd statement considering the length of time they knew each other, but Sydney was way too turned on to think coherently, especially when John began to kneed and kiss her heated flesh. She was so deliciously hot, she couldn't keep still.

"Let's get you out of this," he murmured, tugging at her clothing.

Sydney sat up enough to help him get rid of her top and robe completely. Their movements were frantic and desperate and she could tell by his actions that he craved her as badly as she did him. He was a drug and she was a fiend.

The coolness of the room made her already hard nipples tighten even more. John cupped her breasts in his palms and pushed them together. "Lovely," he murmured. "Your skin is the color of rich dark chocolate, my favorite. My skin against yours, is light against dark, hard against soft and so fucking sexy. Can you imagine it?"

She could. And the thought of the erotic image made her juices flow. Sydney gasped when she felt the warmth of his breath graze her nipples followed by the broad stroke of his tongue.

He circled one taut peak with his tongue before gently suckling it into his mouth. Sydney grasped his head, holding it against her chest. She wiggled beneath him unable to keep still. "Oh John, that feels so good."

He continued to suck her nipples, alternating between them. John was gentle at first, but then his suckles became more aggressive. One of the upsides to being sightless was that she had to depend on her other senses. It wasn't that they'd sharpened or became super human like most people believed, she'd just learned how to use them better. So the feel of his erotic ministrations were even more intense than if she could see. She felt the ridges of his tongue as it swiped her skin, heard his frantic pants, and the scent of his masculinity seemed to get stronger. Sydney had never come from the simple act of having her breasts played with but she was so close she couldn't contain herself.

"John!" she screamed his name as a powerful climax hit her.

He covered her mouth with his again, catching her moans as her body rode the waves of an amazing orgasm. The kiss was hard, passionate and breathtaking. Finally when he broke the tight seal of their lips John stroked her face. "I love how responsive you are. I've dreamed of how you would look like this and you don't disappoint."

Again she found his statement odd but all she could focus on was his hands on her body. John eased her pajama bottoms and panties down her hips before yanking them off completely. "You smell divine, *gattina*. Look at how wet your pussy is. Your juices have soaked your thighs. There's only one thing to be done about this?"

"What?" Her breath hitched in her throat.

John positioned himself between her legs. "I'm going to have to lick you clean. Spread your legs wider so I can taste you properly."

Sydney didn't need to be told twice. John ran his tongue along the insides of her thighs, laving every inch of her skin around her pussy. She lifted her hips, wanting more than his teasing.

"More," she moaned.

He chuckled. "How badly do you want it, Sydney? I want to hear you say it."

"I want it badly. So very bad. Please eat my pussy, John." Was that her voice? So husky and raw with need. She couldn't remember a time when she'd begged for a man to satisfy her sexually. This man seemed to have cast a spell over her.

"I thought you'd never ask," he whispered before bumping his nose against her clit.

"Oh!"

"You liked that?" He did it again, this time following it up with a swipe of his tongue.

Unable to take any more of his teasing she grinded her pussy against his face. "Please," she moaned.

"Mmm, I love the sound of you begging," John murmured before capturing her clit between his lips. As he sucked her hot little button, he slid a finger into her channel. He eased the digit in and out of her.

Sydney rolled her eyes to the back of her head. John's mouth was pure magic. She didn't know how but he made her see colors. As he licked, sucked and stroked her pussy, he thrust another finger inside of her.

"Do you like his, *gattina*? Do you like me eating this delicious pussy? *My* delicious pussy."

One of her biggest turn offs was a man who got too possessive but hearing John's declaration nearly made her melt. The man had somehow cast a spell on her but she didn't care. She was his for the taking. "Love it!" She was so close to reaching her peak again. She clamped her thighs around his head as he ate her pussy like a starving man, so it caught her completely off guard when he sunk his teeth into her inner thighs and began to suck.

"John! What are you doing?"

Instead of answering, he pushed her legs up and positioned them over his knees. He began to make animalistic growling sounds in his throat that frightened and turned her on at the same time.

She pushed at his shoulders but John would not be denied. He lifted his head slightly before burying his face in her pussy. Though she sensed something had changed Sydney didn't have the strength to push him away. She rolled her head from side to side as her body quacked from the way he attacked her pussy.

When her climax came she nearly passed out from the intensity of it but he didn't stop. He finger-fucked, nibbled, sucked and licked her pussy, leaving no part unexplored, and Sydney was helpless to do anything except ride the waves of pleasure that threatened to drown her.

"John, John, John," she chanted over and over again.

It felt like he was between her thighs for hours but finally when she didn't think she take another minute he pulled away from her. She faintly heard the rustling of his clothing before he was on top of her.

"Once we do this, there's no going back," he stated. "I'm going to fuck my tight little pussy until you go hoarse from screaming my name. His voice was deeper and it almost sounded as if he was holding something between his cheeks.

Sydney didn't have a chance to analyze it before he pressed the smooth head of his cock against her pussy. John slid it along her slit, before shoving it past her labia and into her sheath with one powerful thrust.

She wanted to scream but John swallowed it as his mouth covered hers, muffling her cries. Never before had she been so thoroughly stretched, causing a delicious ache that she felt in every single nerve of her body.

John remained still just long enough for her body to adjust to his magnificent size. He kept his mouth pressed firmly against hers as he became to move, slowly at first. He pulled back just until only his tip was inside of her before slamming back into her. He was so deep his balls slapped her ass.

Sydney twisted her head away to catch her breath as she scored her nails down his back. She'd be sore in the morning because of his size and the roughness of his movements but she didn't care. Every time he plowed his cock into her, he hit the spot that made her delirious with pleasure.

"Mine," he growled. "My pussy. So juicy. So good. Perfect just for me." His voice sounded strained but it didn't matter. His dirty talk turned her on more than she ever thought it would.

"Tell me this pussy belongs to me," he growled.

"It's yours, John. All of me is yours." She lifted her hips to meet his thrusts, giving as good as she got. As his cock rammed in and out of her slick sheath, Sydney ran her fingers along his muscular back and just enjoying the feel of his now damp skin beneath her fingertips. John buried his face against her neck as he increased the pace, plowing into her like a man possessed.

She came so hard it felt as if her body had shut down on her. She couldn't move, couldn't think, speak or even remember her name. She'd experienced nirvana, a blissful sensation that made her feel like she was gliding on a cloud that she never wanted to come down from. Sydney could live another hundred years and never feel exactly what she did in this moment.

The slight prick she felt against the area where her neck and shoulder met barely registered. John sucked her flesh, which wasn't an unpleasant feeling.

"Feels….so…good," she whispered before drifting off.

Her blood was like ambrosia, a sweet honeyed nectar he couldn't get enough of. He didn't know what had come over him but once he got that taste of her, he couldn't stop himself. As he continued to drink from her, he noticed that she'd gone still. He could hear her heartbeat which had slowed significantly.

Giovanni pulled back and realized what had happened.

"Shit!"

He rolled off Sydney, ignoring how barren he felt separating from her. She'd gone pale. The usual glow of her beautiful brown skin had dimmed, and her skin had gone cold. If he didn't hear her the faint beat of her heart Giovanni would have thought he'd killed her.

He'd nearly drained her, confirming that his powers were slowly returning. He didn't understand how this could be happening. He had prepared himself to live the rest of his life as a mortal but now he was going through this change at the most inopportune times. This couldn't be happening. Not now.

He had to do something. She needed blood but he couldn't give her his. Considering what she was going through his blood was too unstable. There was no telling the effects it would have on Sydney. If he took her to the hospital there would be way too many questions. He quickly covered her up with his blanket and dropped a kiss on her forehead. Like Sleeping Beauty, she was oblivious to what was going on around her, unaware of his panic. Thankful that his room was one of the few with its own private bathroom Giovanni rushed to it. He took a washcloth and wet it under warm water before returning to Sydney's side.

Carefully, he bathed the sweat, blood and bodily fluid. It was a trial to wash between her legs without losing his mind. His incisors descended again and he couldn't retract them. Heat suffused his body but it wasn't the good kind. Something was happening to him that he couldn't explain. When he finished cleaning Sydney he dressed her but still she remained dead to the world.

He had to revive her soon or he feared she might not wake.

Giovanni knew it was a long shot but he needed to contact Steel who could probably help Sydney.

After throwing on his pajama bottoms, he went through his duffle bag and pulled out the phone he didn't think he'd need to use. It only had a few numbers on it and Steel was one of them. Giovanni prayed that the warlock would answer.

84

He tapped his foot against the floor impatiently as the phone rang on Steel's end but there was no answer. Just when he was on the verge of hanging up there was an answer.

"Giovanni, I'm surprised to hear from you," the warlock greeted.

"I need your help. Right now."

"What can I do for you?"

"Something has gone wrong with the purge. I'm turning back into a vampire."

"Is that a bad thing? We said that being human was possibly temporary."

"I could deal with this if I were able to control my powers. But I can't and something bad has happened."

"What?"

"There's a woman. While we were... Anyway, I took too much blood and now she won't wake up. If I take her to a hospital they may ask too many questions. I don't have access to the database that would tell me what doctors are there who would be discrete about something like this. Is there a way you can get here?"

"Are you in the States?"

"Yes."

Steel let out what sounded like a frustrated sigh. "I'm unfortunately in London at the moment, but the twins are stateside. Give me your address and I'll reach out to them. Hopefully they'll be close to make it there in time. I just need five minutes and I'll call you back to confirm."

"Hurry." Giovanni clicked off without waiting for a response. It was probably rude to end the call so abruptly when he was the one who was in need of help but all he could think of was Sydney.

He rushed back to her side and stroked the side of her face. If he couldn't save her, he not only wouldn't be able to forgive himself, he didn't think he could live with the guilt.

## Chapter Nine

Ten minutes.

He was told the twins would arrive within that time. It was the longest ten minutes in his life. As he waited, Sydney's heartbeat grew fainter. He knelt by the bed with his head pressed against Sydney's body. How could he have lost control like that? One minute he'd experienced his greatest pleasure and the next he was draining her like a savage beast. Holding, kissing and touching Sydney had been beyond anything in his dreams. Not only had the reality lived up to the fantasy, it had surpassed it.

The second he'd slid inside of her he knew without a doubt that she was his bloodmate. Giovanni didn't think he'd ever have one after so many centuries but he'd found her. The problem was, he couldn't claim her. With all the changes going on within him, he didn't know if what happened earlier wouldn't happen again. Besides, he was too damaged. Sydney deserved so much more than he could offer. He'd done too many bad things in his life, hurt a lot of people.

Besides losing Adonis, one of his biggest regrets was hurting his friend Lilianna. She had been a loyal companion over the past several decades. She'd been his confidant, friend and at times, when they both had itches to scratch, his lover. On his end it had never been anything more between them except a strong friendship but Lilianna's feelings for him had been stronger. If he had been a different person, he would have turned her away and allowed her to forge a new path for herself instead of helping him in his pursuits. He'd become so dependent on her help that he'd selfishly kept her around. She would still be alive today if he had only done the right thing.

That was two deaths he had on his hands. How could he move on with his life and find happiness when two people who had meant so much to him couldn't? With that in mind, if the twins could save Sydney, he vowed to leave and never look back. Nya would have to understand. A far as he could tell, Sydney was doing just fine without his interference. While Dylan concerned him, Giovanni figured he could hire someone else to take residence in the house and keep an eye on things in case anything got out of control.

"I see we made it here just in time. Her heartbeat is slowing down."

Giovanni raised his head to see Cutter and Blade Romanov had appeared from out of thin air. Even though they were identical, it was amazing how much alike they looked. Usually there was some kind of identifying detail that made it possible to tell most twins apart but these two were carbon copies of each other. If weren't for the fact that they wore their hair differently, Giovanni wouldn't have known the difference.

He stood up and raked his fingers through his hair in agitation. "It's been more than ten minutes, what took you so long?"

"We were several hundred miles away. Teleporting takes a massive amount of strength and concentration," Cutter, the short-haired twin answered, stepping forward. He walked to where Sydney lay and pressed his hand against her forehead. "We can do a transfusion. Blade and I can infuse some of our blood into her. There will be no side effects besides the healing properties."

Blade joined his brother and took a knee.

Giovanni watched on anxiously as the brothers each took one of Sydney's hands and began to chant in unison. Even though Giovanni had practiced black magic for years it was nothing like the natural powers performed by a witch or warlock. Their joined hands began to glow and the twins fell silent.

Giovanni bit his lip to keep himself from demanding that they hurry but he realized these types of spells took total concentration. All the while he watched anxiously, willing Sydney to give some indication that she would be all right.

After several minutes, Cutter and Blade released her hands and stood. "It's done. It may take a few minutes for her body to restore itself but she shouldn't be any worse for wear once she gains consciousness. We gave her a sleep suggestion at the end of the spell so she won't wake until the sun rises."

Giovanni sat next to Sydney and placed a light kiss on her lips. Words couldn't express how relieved he felt. Because of his fuck up, she could have died. "I'm so sorry," he whispered to her.

Sydney mumbled something in her sleep but other than that she made no other indication that she'd heard him.

He then turned to the two warlocks who looked at them with mild curiosity on their stoic faces. "Thank you. I don't know what I would have done if something happened to her."

Cutter nodded. "You're welcome."

"I'm going to return her to her room."

"It's okay. We'll wait. There's something we need to discuss with you. Don't worry about making too much noise when you take Sydney to her room, the rest of the residents won't wake up until the morning. We placed an enchantment on the house before entering so we wouldn't draw any unwanted attention," Blade explained.

Giovanni was thankful that he'd put Sydney's clothes back on. Even if he had no right to feel this way, it bothered him that anyone else would see her so intimately. Although the twins said they'd put a spell on the house, he was still careful to not make any noise as he delivered Sydney to her room. After gently placing her in the bed, he removed her robe and then tucked her in. He dropped one last kiss on her lips, believing it would be his last.

With a heavy heart, he returned to his room and closed the door behind him. Cutter leaned against the wall, his expression blank, while Blade sat in the chair by the desk. His face was also expressionless. Giovanni didn't know the Romanovs well beyond the time they worked together to take down Adonis and his mother and when they'd helped him with his purge. His connection with them was tenuous at best even though they had a relative in common. But he knew he could trust them. They were strong allies to have in one's corner.

"I can't thank you enough for what you've done tonight, and I apologize for being short with you when the two of you arrived. As I'm sure you could tell, I was frantic with worry for Sydney. I don't know what came over me. I just...as I was telling Steel, one minute I'm having the most incredible experience of my life with her and the next, I'm draining her dry. I've never lacked control like that since I was a baby vampire."

"That makes sense," Blade replied.

Giovanni raised a brow. "What do you mean it makes sense? What are you talking about? This wasn't one of the things we discussed before you performed the spell on me."

"I know," the warlock continued. "We told you all that we knew about it at the time. It's not something that's commonly used. To my recollection, the purge has only ever been done as a counter spell; usually one who has practiced the dark arts for as long as you have doesn't willingly volunteer to relinquish their powers. As far as any of us knew the two biggest possibilities would be death or you becoming mortal. Whether that mortality was permanent couldn't be determined at the time."

Cutter pushed himself from the wall and walked to the center of the room. "We wanted to research it further just in case something were to occur."

"Well it did," Giovanni interrupted. "What did you find out?"

Cutter exchanged a look with his brother before answering. "What we learned was that the length of mortality depended on whether you were born or made a vampire. Since you were made, it should have been longer. When Steel told us what had happened it baffled us, but then we figured it might be because you're over seven hundred years old. You've been a vampire far longer than you've been human. But there's also another factor that we didn't piece together until we saw you with your Sydney. You know that mates are important to immortals. When we find our mates, we find the other half of our souls. It's clear she's your bloodmate and meeting her might have sparked your body into these changes prematurely. What's likely to happen is you'll gain all your powers back, your strength, the heightened senses and so forth. But there will be some complications."

"I've already experience them. Didn't you see what I did to her? I couldn't fucking control myself."

"Exactly," Cutter agreed. "As you regain your abilities you won't be able to manage them at first. They'll grow erratic. You vampires have a thing you suffer through when you're denied the thing you most require."

"*La morte dolci,*" Giovanni whispered. He'd never experienced it before but he'd seen other vampires suffer from it. It wasn't pretty and often times those dealing with it left a trail of destruction in their wake. This definitely firmed his resolve to leave here and never look back. He couldn't trust himself to be in this house and put Sydney in danger. He released a heavy sigh. "Do you know how long it will last?"

"We're not sure," Blade answered. "It could take a few days or even weeks."

"Okay." Giovanni took a seat on his bed and dropped his head into his hands. He wasn't sure how he felt about becoming a vampire again. Despite being one for most of his life he believed that being human would be part of his punishment, but now he would once again live forever. He couldn't take his own life because that would be the easy way out. He deserved every bit of misery coming his way. "Well, I thank you both for coming and helping me out of my predicament. I should probably start packing my belongings. I need to get out of here before Sydney stirs."

Blade stood up. "I know why you feel you have to leave but there may be a reason why you should stay."

Giovanni shook her head. "Don't tell me I have to stay for Sydney's sake. She's the reason I have to go. I can't place her in danger again. Tonight was just a preview of what I'm capable of. The next time you two might not be around to bail me out of trouble."

"Maybe not but there's a good reason why you should stay. I'd only recommend going if you place someone in the house who you trust," Cutter countered.

Though it was Giovanni's plan to do just that, there seemed to be urgency in the warlock's words. "Why?"

"You probably don't feel it because your full powers haven't returned, but there's dark magic here. In this house. I can't tell the source unless we do a thorough inspection from top to bottom, but it's powerful and if I'm not mistaken, someone has already used it on Sydney. When I touched her there was something distorted in her spirit. A malevolent force means her harm. I understand you want to keep away from Sydney but someone should keep an eye on her."

His heart raced. Who here could possibly want to harm Sydney? Other than Dylan the rest of the boarders seemed harmless. Now he understood why Nya had sent him here. She must have felt it too when she had last seen Sydney. "Fuck," he muttered under his breath. "This is why Nya wanted me to come here."

Both twins seemed to come to life at the mention of his friend's name. "You've seen Nya? What does she have to do with all this?" Blade demanded.

"Has she been here?" Cutter questioned him sounding every bit as eager as his brother.

When they'd last spoke, Nya had mentioned the twins being a bit of a thorn in her side. It was obvious their interest in her wasn't simply mild curiosity.

"I spoke to her some weeks ago. She's the reason I'm here. Nya has been keeping an eye on Sydney and her family for years. They were her last living descendants so she had a vested interest to look out for them. Then when Sydney lost her family Nya became even more protective of her, but she had to stop her visits because Adonis was having her watched. So she entrusted me to keep an eye on Sydney. I watched her like I promised I would but when I first saw Sydney, I couldn't approach her like I told Nya I would. I think even then I knew she was my bloodmate. I couldn't complicate my life at the time. I felt that just keeping tabs on her was sufficient even though I told Nya that I had actually met Sydney first hand to reassure her. The last time I talked to her, she was insistent that I come down here and pose as a boarder. She wouldn't tell me why, but she must have sensed something the last time she was here."

"But you didn't feel it during your last visit?" Cutter asked. "You were still a vampire then were you not?"

"I was but like I said, I kept my distance. Nya has actually been inside this house. She pretended to be a salesperson so it gave her an opportunity to speak with Sydney. Nya didn't elaborate beyond that."

"And have you spoken to Nya lately?" Blade wanted to know.

"No. I'm not sure when I'll see her again, but she knows how to get in contact with me."

"Do you know how to get in contact with her?" Blade persisted.

Giovanni raised a brow. "Even if I did, I wouldn't share that information. Look, it didn't escape my notice the last time we were all together that you two have taken an interest in her but you've got to know, she was

Adonis's bloodmate. She's still dealing with that. You two are going to have to give her time."

Cutter flared his nostrils obviously not pleased with Giovanni's words. "How much time would you suggest?"

"As much time as she needs. And for the record, she's worth more than just a fling so if that's all you two have in mind where she's concerned I'd suggest you leave her alone."

Blade narrowed his eyes to ice blue slits. "You seem to have a pretty low opinion of us considering you just needed our help."

"And I appreciate what you've done. But Nya is my friend. I've known her for a long time. She might wear a tough exterior but on the inside she's quite sensitive. I will not have either of you hurt her."

Cutter crossed the room to stand in front of Giovanni. "Trust us when we say that's the last thing we'd ever do to her. We've been looking for her actually. But we lost her trail a few weeks ago. It's like she vanished into thin air."

Giovanni shrugged. "When she wants to be found, she'll make an appearance. She has connections who can help her disappear if she so chooses."

The twins looked at each other and shared a secret look. By the time they returned their attention to Giovanni, he felt like they had secretly communicated something to each other. "Well, we should be going, but should you need us, we'll leave our numbers. And if we don't answer right away, you can always contact Steel or our sister, who has a way of reaching us without technology," Blade instructed.

"Wait!" Giovanni stood. He didn't want them to disappear just yet. "What should I do? Am I supposed to wait this thing out? Is there a spell you can perform to make this thing I'm going through vanish?"

They shook their heads simultaneously but Blade spoke. "This is something that will need to run its course. Sydney was the catalyst for you getting your powers back so quickly so maybe she's also the key to you getting over *la morte dolci*. In the meantime, find out where the source of the dark power is coming from or else your transformation won't be the only issue."

"That's it?"

"Don't be afraid to ask for help, Giovanni," Cutter answered before vanishing with his twin.

As Giovanni stood alone in his room he realized he was well and truly fucked.

## Chapter Ten

The unwelcome sound of her alarm clock, jarringly brought Sydney out of a peaceful sleep. Normally she had no problem getting out of bed in the morning but she felt a bit sluggish and every single muscle in her body ached, even in places she didn't know she had them. Most of all she was sore between her legs as if…

She sat up abruptly. It all came back to her. She'd had sex with John! She wasn't sure how it had happened but one minute they were talking about his nightmares and the next minute she was in bed with him begging to be taken. Her face grew hot from embarrassment as she thought of all the things they'd done and what she'd allowed him to do to her. He'd worked his tongue in ways that probably would have put a porn star to shame.

She wasn't sure what was worse, breaking her own rule about keeping a professional distance between herself and her boarders, or the fact that John Chandler was still basically a stranger. She hadn't known him that long, and what did she actually know about him she'd learned through the agency she used to do background checks. Sure he'd shared some information on the brother he'd lost, but that didn't exactly mean she was well-versed in John's life.

She didn't know what made him tick, what it had been like for him growing up, his favorite color, just basic things one should learn about a person before jumping in bed with them. But yet she felt a pull to him that she couldn't explain. Whenever she was in his presence, besides the overwhelming lust she experienced, he had a calming effect on her. She felt safe. Still, what had happened between them shouldn't have.

Sydney was absolutely mortified at her own behavior and she wasn't exactly sure how she would face him, or anyone else in the house for that matter. It wasn't as if they'd been quiet. They'd probably awoken a few people.

What would Ida say? She was certain her friend wouldn't be quiet on the matter. And then there was Dylan to contend with. She'd already decided that she would ask him to leave the house. Now that would be nearly impossible to do. The last thing Sydney wanted to do was make waves with Ida when she herself had screwed up so badly.

But the worst part was that if she could do it all again, there was no doubt in her mind that she would. Even though the situation had been wrong, it had felt oh so right. Even now as she thought about it now, heat rushed to her core.

As much as Sydney wanted to wallow in bed for the rest of the day and avoid everyone, she had things to do around the house. Sydney winced as she slid out of bed. It suddenly occurred to her that John must have returned her to her bedroom. She remembered passing out in his room after the most incredible orgasm she'd even experienced. Her pajamas were back on, so he must have dressed her as well. She squirmed at the thought of his hands on her body. Sydney wondered if he'd touched her while she was unconscious. Somehow that thought turned her on way more than it shoulder have. As she moved toward the bathroom to wash up, her body ached, but it was a nice kind of ache that could only come from sexual exertion.

Once she was under her shower's spray she could think more coherently, but that didn't help much because all her thoughts centered on John, on her and inside of her. Sydney moaned as she soaped her body, imagining that it was John in the stall with her, caressing her body and making her feel more alive than she had in years.

She cupped her breasts in her palms and tweaked her nipples. "John," she whispered his name, remembering what it felt like to have his hands on her body. Slowly, she eased one hand down the center of her body and slipped a finger inside her throbbing pussy. She planted her other hand against the wall to support herself as she worked her finger in and out of her now dripping channel. She wiggled and squirmed, her hips pushing herself to a quick climax. Sydney leaned against the wall to catch her breath.

This had to stop. Somehow she was going to have to stay away from John or else she might have to give him a refund on his rent and tell him to leave. There didn't seem to be any other solution.

By the time she made her way downstairs Ida was already in the kitchen fixing breakfast. Sydney walked to the fridge to get some orange juice as was her morning ritual. "Good morning, Ida," she greeted, feeling unsure about the reception she would receive. Ida wasn't one to bite her tongue so if she'd heard anything the night before the older woman wouldn't be hesitant to say it.

"Morning," Ida mumbled.

"I was going to start breakfast, but I see you beat me to it. Is there anything I can help you with?"

"No. I've got it under control. I'm surprised you're even up this early considering the night you had." Ida's words dripped with accusation and Sydney could hear her friend's disappointment.

"Ida, look—"

"Sydney, you don't have to explain anything to me. You're welcome to live your life how you choose. If you want to sleep around that's on you, but I'd think you'd be a little more discreet considering we have a houseful of people. Anyway, I thought you were a little more sensitive than that."

Sydney sighed. She'd prepared herself for Ida's lecture but hearing this scathing dismissal made her feel even guiltier. "I'm sorry to have caused such a disturbance. It won't happen again."

Ida snorted. "You're worried about the noise? That's all you care about? That you might have interrupted people's sleep? If it were only that I could overlook it but you know Dylan is in the house and you know how he feels about you. Did you think about what you might be doing to him?"

Now it was Sydney's turn to get angry. Yes, she was wrong for what she did with John, but she owed nothing to Dylan. "Dylan has nothing to do with this because he and I aren't together. That didn't work out, remember? Because he nearly killed someone for just talking to me. And I wish you would stop acting like that was some minor offense. He's lucky he's not rotting somewhere in a prison cell. The fact that I even allow him in my house after that is because of you and for no other reason. Dylan and I are never going to be a thing ever again. That's a mistake I don't intend to repeat. And furthermore—Argh!" Sydney clutched her head as she felt a sharp stabbing pain in her head.

She fell to her knees because the ache was almost unbearable.

"Sydney!" Ida was at her side immediately. "Are you okay?"

Sydney couldn't think or move. The pain was paralyzing. "Head," she managed to whisper. "Hurts."

"I'm going to call 911. Just hold tight."

Sydney wanted to shake her head no but the slightest movement was jarring. It had been a struggle to get her last two words out. The throbbing in her head seemed to spread throughout her entire body, making her wish she was dead.

Giovanni had every intention of being gone by the time the sun rose, but his conversation with Cutter and Blade had got him to thinking. Though they didn't specify what the dark force was, it could have been any number of things. Giovanni decided he couldn't leave Sydney vulnerable to it, at least not until someone else was here to take his place.

There were very few people he trusted for that task. He'd employed many over the years to aid him in the task of protecting his brothers but he wasn't particularly close to any of them. If he knew of her whereabouts, he'd contact Nya to come and check on Sydney herself, after all this was her relative. He thought about reaching out to Dante and his other brothers but that wouldn't have been fair. They were all leading happy lives and the last thing he wanted to do was involve them in his problems. It wasn't as if he had the right to anyway.

After the twins had left, Giovanni wasn't sure what to do with himself so he left the house to go for a long walk. The one thing about the southern region of US that he liked was how quiet everything was at night. Unlike the big cities where the hustle and bustle never stopped, he enjoyed the stillness giving one the ability to reflect and meditate.

Giovanni must have walked for hours and had even crossed the city limits as he contemplated his next move. He could ask the twins to come back and do a more thorough search of the house to figure out where the source of the danger lurked but he'd already called in so many favors with the Romanovs he couldn't ask them for help yet again.

And there within lay his dilemma. He couldn't trust himself around Sydney until he was fully himself again. It would kill him if he hurt her in any way. Once had been enough. When he thought he'd killed her, it felt like his world was caving in on him. He couldn't take it if he'd actually succeeded.

As he walked the night it struck him how utterly alone he felt. He didn't count the handful of people in his life that he occasionally associated with, he meant in the here and now. He wasn't close to his brothers and his one good friend was missing in action. If he were to die tonight would anyone really care? Would he be mourned? He realized he'd spent most of his life in isolation, and he wondered if his reluctance to reach out to anyone for help was because he was just so used to going it alone. He remembered one of the last cordial conversations he had with Adonis which brought that to mind. It had been sometime around the ninetieth century and it was the first time he actually faced the idea that it might be too late to save his brother.

*"You know you're wasting your time trying to save them."*

*Giovanni sat before the fire place, sipping on an Irish whiskey he'd grown fond of. Though he wasn't capable of getting drunk, it gave him a nice warm feeling inside. And for the rare moments when he forced himself to relax, it served to calm his nerves. Though he was surprised by his brother's appearance, he didn't want to give too much away. They hadn't had a proper conversation in years.*

*"What brings you to this part of the world? I thought you hated Venice."*

*"I never said I hated it. I would prefer a warmer climate. Besides, I'd rather walk on dry land than to be constantly navigating my way around in a boat."*

*A smile titled Giovanni's lips. It wasn't his favorite thing either but he'd purchased this house because it put him in close proximity to the ones he wanted to keep an eye on. "To what do I owe the pleasure of your visit, Adonis? We haven't spoken in years. As a matter of fact I do believe the last time we talked you called me a traitor for foiling your plan, so I'm sure you didn't come to exchange pleasantries."*

*Adonis walked further into the room and took the seat directly across from Giovanni. "You sound so sure of that."*

*"As sure as I know that when you walk out this door, it will be a very long time when we next speak."*

*"Perhaps that's something we should amend."*

*Giovanni raised a brow in surprise. "What's changed from the last time we spoke? Have you decided to drop this vendetta you have against our younger brothers?"*

*Adonis narrowed his golden eyes and flared his nostrils. "They are no brothers of mine."*

*Giovanni sighed. Adonis refused to acknowledge the offspring their natural father Gio had produced with his bloodmate. During that last visit with the Don's sisters and cousins, there had been an upheaval in their home when their mother had been caught in a compromising position with Gio, their stable master.*

*Fabricio brought forth the charge that Beatrice was not only an adulteress, but the sons she had borne were not the Don's. Once people acknowledged the uncanny resemblance he and Adonis had to Gio, it was hard to deny. It all made sense as to Giovanni why he'd felt so close to the stable master. Gio was his true papa, and it made him happy knowing he had no blood ties to Don Sarducci. Adonis, being the favored one, however, was devastated by the news. He was no longer the son of a powerful Duca. He was the bastard son of a servant and a whore who'd managed to wiggle her way into a nobleman's affections.*

*Giovanni, Adonis and Beatrice were thrown off the estate with only the clothes on their backs. The villagers who once revered them and bowed whenever they rode through town, would now whisper behind their backs, throw things at them and spit on them. They had to rely on the kindness of strangers to get by those first few years. It was during that time when Giovanni and Adonis had clung to each other but it was also marked the change in Adonis's personality. Their mother began to toy with Adonis's mind. Since Giovanni and Beatrice had never been close it was difficult for her to manipulate him.*

*Giovanni cared for his mother for the simple fact that she'd given birth to him, but he saw right through her. She was a selfish woman who would do anything and use anyone to get what she wanted, even her own son. He watched helplessly as Beatrice manipulated and brainwashed Adonis into believing things that simply weren't reality. The laughing, generous boy that Adonis had once been became the man before him now. He was cold, callous and a murderer. Despite this, Giovanni refused to give up hope that he could help Adonis see the error of his ways.*

*"Let's not argue, Adonis. Tell me, why did you come here?"*

*"Would you believe it's because I wanted to talk?"*

*"That's odd you'd seek me out after nearly a century. What did you have in mind?"*

*Adonis hesitated, a look of uncertainty crossed his face and in that very moment Giovanni caught a glance of the brother he once know. It was just as he thought, Adonis was still in there somewhere. "I think about how we would talk all night until the sun rose. We'd be so exhausted during our lessons we could barely keep our eyes open."*

*A smile touched Giovanni's lips. "Yes. I remember. And when we'd fall asleep during the lessons, our instructor would rap our knuckles with a cane."*

*"Remember when I hid that cane? He was furious."*

*Giovanni chuckled. "Yes. I remember."*

*"We had good times then."*

*"We did."*

*"We made a good team and it pains me that we find ourselves on different sides of this war."*

*Giovanni lowered his head with a sigh. "It doesn't have to be a war, Adonis. We can both be on the same side."*

*"I'm glad you said that because I was thinking the same thing. Every time I make a move, you counter it and vice versa. It hurts. I don't want to fight my best friend anymore."*

*This is all Giovanni ever wanted to hear from his brother. These past several decades had not only been a physical trial but a mental and spiritual one as well. It was tearing him apart. Adonis's words echoed Giovanni's thoughts. He didn't want to fight his brother. But what kept him going was the knowledge that he was doing the right thing. "It means a lot to me to hear you say that. Let's put the past behind us and start fresh. We can have the life we always wanted, away from all the unnecessary chaos and away from Beatrice."*

*Adonis stiffened at the mention of their mother's name. "Why would we be away from her? She is our mother. The woman who sacrificed so much to raise us. Do you think it was easy for her when the Don kicked us out? Or how about when her youngest son abandoned us? You left us without a backward glance to go to* that *man."*

*"That man is our father. He loves us."*

"He's brainwashed you. He took advantage of our mother and forced himself on her. If it weren't for that whore Maria then he would have died a long time ago. But I suppose she did me a favor because I had the honor of killing him myself for what he did to our mother."

"You actually believe that story our mother told? You and I both know that no one can force Beatrice to do something she doesn't want to. She seduced him."

"She – " Adonis broke off and shook his head. "I didn't come here to argue with you. I came to forgive you of your transgressions. Our mother is willing to do the same. If you combine your powers with ours, we'll be an unstoppable force."

Adonis felt his heart drop. "So this was it. You didn't come because you missed me. You just want to use me to implement your plan for world domination." Realizing that hurt Giovanni more than Adonis could ever know.

"No. I want you to join us because I care. I meant everything I said. I miss you and we should be fighting on the same side."

"But what exactly are you fighting for, Adonis? To complete a vendetta that shouldn't be? You've already killed our father and Maria. You killed GianMarco's wife and child. And I regret that I couldn't get to there in time to save any of them. But I vow that you will not hurt our brothers. I'll make sure of it." Giovanni glared at Adonis, feeling a mixture of anger, pain and regret.

Adonis slowly rose. His eyes started to change to a deep red. "So you choose them over me? They don't even know you exist but you go against your own brother to protect them?"

Giovanni jumped to his feet to stand nose to nose with Adonis. "They're our brothers too! And you've spent years tormenting them. And why? Because of the whims of a mad woman!"

Adonis's face turned as red as his hair. "Don't speak of our mother like that!"

106

*"She is insane. The dark magic has warped her beyond the point of no return even though she barely had any redeeming qualities to begin with. What she did to you —"*

*"Shut up!" Adonis pushed Giovanni with a force that sent him stumbling backward but he managed to stay on his feet.*

*Giovanni wouldn't back down from this because it needed to be said. "What she did to you was unnatural. She changed you. How else can you justify going after innocents? How can you go after our brothers when they've done nothing to you?"*

*Adonis advanced on him but Giovanni was ready. He deflected the blow that came his way and flashed across the room. "Stop this Adonis. This isn't you!"*

*"Fuck you, Giovanni! You know nothing about me. I made a mistake coming here. I shouldn't have expected you to see reason. You speak of insignificant beings as if I should feel some connection to them. When I think of those who you would call brother, I think of that man who betrayed our mother. It was because of him that we were discarded without a penny to our name. He did that to us and while we suffered he lived blissfully with his whore. I hate him ad everything that he stood for. I have no regrets for what I did. I want to wipe out everything he ever loved. I will burn his legacy to the ground. And if you continue to stand in my way, Giovanni, I won't hesitate to take you out too. This will be the last time I come to you" And with that, Adonis flashed away.*

*It was then when Giovanni realized he was all alone.*

As he made it back to the house he noticed an ambulance and a handful of police vehicles in the driveway. He ran up to the driveway just in time to see the paramedics wheel Sydney into the back of the vehicle.

## Chapter Eleven

Sydney woke up in unfamiliar surroundings. This wasn't her bed. It was way too hard. She reached out and encountered railings. There was a steady beeping noise. She struggled to sit up, but was pushed back down. "You need to rest. You gave us quite a scare, Sydney," Ida said.

"Where am I?"

"At the hospital. You came to in the ambulance but then you went out again. I was so worried about you."

"The hospital? Why am I here?"

"Don't you remember anything, sweetheart?"

Sydney struggled to recall the events that would have led up to her being here. "I felt a stabbing pain in my head, like a migraine but way more intense. I couldn't move. It felt like something was trying to take control of me. And now I'm here. How long have you been here?"

"I've been here the entire time. Someone had come by to get some papers signed while you were unconscious but you don't have to worry about them. I took the liberty of signing them for you."

"How were you able to do that?"

"I had to tell the administrators that you were my granddaughter so they could tell me what was going on with you. Something about HIPPA."

"What did they say?"

"You had an irregular heartbeat and your blood pressure was sky high. You're lucky you didn't have a stroke. That probably explains why you suffered that pain in your head."

"I've had headaches before but nothing like that."

"The doctors were able to stabilize you and they can't find anything else the matter but they want to run some more tests. You really had me worried, Sydney. One minute we were arguing and the next you're passed out on the floor."

She furrowed her brow. "We were arguing?"

"Yes, and I just wanted to say I'm sorry for what I said. You're an adult capable of making your own decisions and I was out of line to butt my nose into your business."

Sydney scratched her head. She had no idea what Ida was talking about. She tried to remember the argument in question but as she attempted to bring the memory back, her head began to hurt. The harder she tried to recall it, the worse the pain got. She clutched her head.

"Sydney! What's wrong? Should I call the doctor?"

Sydney took several breaths to manage the pain. Only when she forced herself to relax did it subside. Finally when she was able to answer, she shook her head. "I'm fine, but I don't remember us arguing."

Ida patted her on the arm. "Then don't worry about it. It wasn't important anyway. Just concentrate on getting better. In the meantime, I'll stay with you. I'm not going anywhere."

"Thank you, Ida. You're a good friend. But you don't have to stay here with me. I don't want to put you out." Sydney sunk into her pillow with an uneasy feeling settling over her.

"Believe me, this is no trouble at all. I know we can butt heads sometimes but you're not just a friend to me. You're family and families look out for each other. Just know that no matter what I'll always have your best interests at heart."

Sydney found that last sentence odd but she didn't dwell on it. She was still trying to figure out what was going on. Why couldn't she remember what happened to her earlier? "Ida, how long have I been out?"

"Only for a few hours. It's still a little after two now."

"Who's watching the house?"

"I told Dylan to keep an eye on things. I hope you don't mind."

"Dylan?" Sydney felt as if she should be upset about that but she couldn't bring herself to worry about that."

"It's not a problem, is it?"

"Umm, no. It's fine."

"Are you feeling up to eating anything?"

"Honestly I don't have much of an appetite. I don't mean to sound ungrateful but I'd really like to be alone right now."

Ida didn't answer at first. "Just go to sleep. I won't disturb you."

"No. Please, Ida I'd rather be by myself right now."

Ida took Sydney's hand and rubbed the back of it. "Just relax. I'll call the doctor so he can give you some painkillers that will help you sleep." Ida released her hand and seemed to rummage around for something. "There. Someone will be on their way to check in on you."

She wasn't sure why Ida didn't want to leave her side. Maybe it was guilt because of the argument Sydney still couldn't remember.

Pulling her hand out of Ida's, Sydney turned to her side, careful not to jostle the IV in her hand.

There was a knock on the door, indicating she had a visitor.

"Come in," Ida answered.

"Ms. Lewis? Are you awake?"

Sydney opened her eyes and turned her head toward the sound of her visitor's voice. "Yes, I'm up."

"Good. You pressed the help button for a nurse but as I was on my way to your room I decided to find out what we can do for you. I'm Dr. Green, by the way." He sounded friendly enough.

"I didn't need anything actually but I do have some questions."

"Of course."

"What's the matter with me?"

"Right now you're just fine. When you were admitted I was worried about your blood pressure but we've got that under control. You had an irregular heartbeat as well but that too is back to normal. I'd like to do some further tests and if everything checks out, I'm recommending that you stay overnight for observation but in the morning we can discharge you."

"Dr. Green, the kind of pain I experienced doesn't seem like it would be caused by high blood pressure."

"Believe me Ms. Lewis, high blood pressure can cause a various number of ailments, but I've ordered a CAT scan for you later today to make sure nothing else is going on with you. Someone will also be by to get a blood sample. Are you still feeling any pain?"

"I was a few minutes before you came in but I'm fine now."

"I'll have a nurse come with some pain meds. You can take them as needed. Do you have any other questions for me?"

Sydney wasn't sure but an unsettling feeling took a hold of her that she couldn't shake. "No. Thanks."

"Good. I'll be making my rounds again later this evening. Until then, take care."

Once the doctor left, Sydney turned on her side. "I'm going to try to go back to sleep."

"You go ahead. I'll be right here."

That statement should have made Sydney feel better but she just couldn't rid herself of that uneasy sensation. What was wrong with her?

Giovanni was frantic with worry by the time he made it to the hospital. Even though he'd vowed to stay away from Sydney, his resolve flew out the window the second he saw her being driven away by the ambulance; he had to see her if for nothing else than to reassure himself that she was okay. It felt as if his entire world was crumbling and he was helpless to do anything about it. He wondered if it was the dark force that was responsible for her need of medical assistance. Several scenarios raced through his mind and none of them were good.

Because 'John Chandler' didn't own a vehicle, he had to wait for a cab to take him to his destination. He made it to the hospital only to be denied entrance to Sydney's room. According to the nurse, Sydney's grandmother had said she was to have no visitors. As far as he knew, Sydney had no family. It was times like these when his former powers would have come in handy. He could have glamored the nurse to tell him what room Sydney was in. As luck would have it, however, he spotted Ida coming out of one of the rooms and it dawned on Giovanni that she must have told the staff that she was Sydney's grandmother. Why she'd want to keep any visitors from seeing Sydney was beyond him but at least one mystery was solved.

He quickly ducked behind a column as Ida came toward him. Just as she was about to pass him, she paused and looked around her with a frown as if sensing she was being watched. Giovanni scooted away, making sure she didn't see him. Finally when she began to walk again and was around the corner he released a deep sigh of relief. Sneaking past the nurse's station, he hurried down the hallway to the room Ida had just vacated.

He quickly entered without knocking. Giovanni's breath caught in his throat when he saw Sydney lying in the bed, hooked up to an IV, looking so helpless and small. Her eyes were closed and he assumed she was asleep. As he approached her bedside, his heart raced. Unable to help himself, he reached out and grazed her cheek with the back of his hand.

Her eyes slowly drifted open. "John?"

Giovanni yanked his hand back. "I thought you were sleeping."

"No, I was just pretending. I thought you were Ida. She went to the cafeteria because I told her I wanted a soda. It was the only way I could think to get rid of her."

"Why would you want to get rid of her?"

"She was smothering me. I know she means well, but I just wanted a few moments by myself."

"Then maybe I should go too. I came because I wanted to see how you're doing."

As he backed away, she stretched her hand out to him but didn't quite connect. "Please. Don't go. I don't mind if you stay for a bit."

"Are you sure?"

"Yes. Please take a seat. I may not be able to see you hovering over me, but I can hear you fidgeting. You're making me feel self-conscious."

"Sorry." He took the seat closest to her bed. "How are you feeling?"

"Fine now. It was a bit scary waking up in the hospital and not knowing what was going on. Ida explained to me that we were having an argument of some kind and I passed out. I don't remember any of it. The doctor says my blood pressure skyrocketed. They're going to run some more tests but he doesn't seem to think they'll find anything. It could be just one of those freak things. I did have a bit of a headache earlier but I'm okay now."

Giovanni frowned not liking the sound of that. "What is the last thing you remembered before coming to?"

"Honestly? I remember us going for a walk. And I enjoyed it, probably a little too much."

He froze. She couldn't be serious. "You remember nothing else? Not last night?"

She scrunched her face as if she was trying to concentrate before clutching her head. "Oh."

"What's the matter?" he asked in panic.

"The headache is coming back. Every time I try to remember what happened my head starts throbbing."

"Our walk is the last thing you remember?" he asked incredulously.

"Yes. You sound surprised."

"I am because that happened last week."

She moved to a sitting position, her mouth agape. "What? Are you sure?"

"I'm positive. You're telling me you've lost the last several days?" He wasn't sure if he was relieved or dismayed that she didn't remember a thing about the night before. While it had probably meant more to him than anything he'd ever experienced, he was glad at the very least that she also lost the memory of him losing control. Briefly he wondered if this was a side effect of the Romanovs' spell but immediately dispelled the idea. They were far too experienced to allow something like this to happen. Was it like Sydney's doctor suggested, that it was a one-time incident, or was there more to it like the dark force that had been alluded to?

Her symptoms sounded vaguely familiar but he couldn't think of where he'd seen them before.

"I don't know how that could be. The doctor didn't mention it...but then again, I didn't know."

"You should tell him about it when he comes to the room again. In the meantime you need to lie down and rest."

She shook her head. "I've been resting since I've been here. Actually you and I should talk."

Something in Sydney's tone told Giovanni that he wouldn't necessarily like what she had to say. "Okay? What did you want to talk about?"

"That kiss."

"The kiss? I thought you didn't rememb—oh, when we went for our walk."

"Yes. I...I don't know where to begin." She let out a nervous giggle. "I'm not going to lie John. I enjoyed that kiss. Probably more than I should have. From the moment I met you, I felt this connection I couldn't quite explain and in other circumstances, I wouldn't be averse to exploring where things could go with us. But you're my boarder and I don't think it's a good idea to get involved. Besides, I haven't had much success in the love department. Knowing my luck even if something did happen between us it would end badly. I can't take that risk. I mean, I am wildly attracted to you but this thing between us just can't happen."

Giovanni wasn't in a position to act on his feelings for her until his transformation was complete and he figured out the danger that surrounded her. Still, her words were like a kick in his gut. Making love to her meant absolutely everything to him and it hurt his ego and heart that she didn't remember, but perhaps it was for the best.

"John?"

He opened his mouth to speak but the words wouldn't come. He wanted to pull her in his arms and fuck her senseless and make her remember their night together, but he managed to push that impulse away.

"Oh my God." She lowered her head. "I'm so embarrassed. I read too much into that kiss, didn't I?"

He realized that she'd misinterpreted his silence. "No. That's not it at all. I enjoyed the kiss, Sydney. More than you could know. You're a beautiful, accomplished woman. And I'd like nothing more than to pursue a relationship with you, but the timing is off. I'm going to have to go away for a while."

"What?"

"I have to leave. It's for the best."

Just then, the door opened. Ida walked in and if looks could kill he'd be dead on the spot. "What the hell are you doing here?"

## Chapter Twelve

Sydney had never heard her friend sound so angry. Why did Ida have a problem with her having visitors? She knew Ida didn't care for John but she wouldn't allow the woman to dictate who she could talk to. "He's visiting me," she spoke up.

"Yes," John added. "And I was just leaving. I was also telling Sydney that I'll have to go away for a while, so I'll be out of your hair, Ida."

"Good," the older woman muttered. "You've been nothing but trouble since you got to the house."

"Ida! You're being rude!" Sydney gasped as a sudden sharp pain sliced through her head. It disappeared as quickly as it came but it made her fall against her pillow in agony.

"What's wrong, Sydney?" John demanded, sounding frantic.

"You're what's wrong," Ida argued. "You're stressing her out. You're not supposed to be here."

Sydney moistened her suddenly dry lips with the tip of her tongue. "Ida I know you're just looking out for me, but I'm perfectly capable of speaking for myself. It was just a pain in my head. It felt like I was about to get a migraine but it went away."

"Maybe you should rest."

Sydney rubbed her temples, fearful the pain would come back.

"Sydney, do you want me to go?" John asked.

She remembered that he'd told her only a few minutes earlier. "Weren't you about to leave anyway? John, you don't have to worry, I'll be okay. Thank you for visiting me. It means a lot."

"You heard her." Ida sucked her teeth. "She's not up to having visitors."

Sydney would have said something under any other circumstances but she felt tired and weak all of a sudden. She simply didn't have the energy to play referee. "Yes, John. Maybe you should go."

He didn't respond immediately. "Okay."

To her surprise, she could feel John's heat as he seemed to get closer and closer and then he kissed her forehead. His lips were so warm they nearly burned. Despite this, a shiver that was akin to an electric wave vaulted through her. It felt familiar and she didn't understand why.

"John, are you feeling well?" she asked.

"I'm fine," came his hoarse response.

"You're burning up. Maybe you should see the doctor before you leave the hospital."

"I'll be okay. I'm going now. I'm still paid up for another couple of months at the house so you may hear from me before then. If not, take care of yourself, Sydney."

"And don't forget to take your stuff with you," Ida interjected rudely.

"Ida!" Sydney was more than a little annoyed at her friend's hostility toward John.

"Well, we're not a storage facility," the woman muttered.

"Goodbye, Sydney."

Those were John's last words before she heard the door open and then close again, indicating that he'd left the room. She didn't understand why, but Sydney felt a little sad, and betrayed by the fact that he was leaving without notice. He was free to come and go as he pleased and she had no right to want him to stick around but she did. There had been a connection between them that she couldn't quite explain, but it was strong and under different circumstances it might have been something she would have pursued.

And then there was that kiss. Suddenly the memory of him pressing his body against hers, and slipping into her wetness caught her off guard. It seemed so real but she was sure that didn't happen. She would have remembered having sex with him.

"Sydney, are you listening to me?" Ida snapped her fingers near Sydney's ear, interrupting her thoughts.

"I'm sorry. What were you saying?"

Ida exhaled deeply, probably from frustration. "I've been trying to get your attention for the past couple minutes. You were daydreaming. Were you thinking about that man?"

Irritated by Ida's tone Sydney grimaced. "And if I was? Are you trying to control my thoughts?"

"There's no need to get snippy. I'm just concerned. I told you I had a bad feeling about that guy and now I know why. I did a little asking around town. Folks have told me that they've seen him around these parts before. Said he was watching you."

Sydney snorted. "That's ridiculous. John is new to town. Most of our boarders have heard of us through the online ad. I think they must be mistaken."

"Or maybe that man is stalking you." Ida took Sydney's hand and began to stroke it. "Look, I'm probably being a silly old woman but the only reason I get like this sometimes is because I care. Sydney, you're like a daughter to me and I'm just looking out for you."

Ida's words seemed to have a calming effect on her. Her friend had never let her down before and if it was true what she said about John did that mean she should be worried? She didn't want to believe it but how well did she know the man beyond what he'd told her. How much of it was truth if any? "Maybe you're right Ida, but seeing that he's gone for God knows how long, the point is moot. For all we know he may never come back."

"It would be better if he didn't," Ida mumbled but then quickly added, "Dylan is on his way over to visit."

Sydney stiffened. She wasn't sure why Dylan's name caused her so much anxiety, after all he was a nice enough guy. She rubbed her forehead when it began to throb again. "Dylan? Didn't you just tell John to leave because you didn't want me to have any visitors?"

Ida made a sucking sound. "Oh, I just didn't want *that* man upsetting you."

Sydney sighed, not having the strength to argue. The sporadic pain in her head was quickly becoming a concern. "Maybe you should tell him to come another time."

"Nonsense." Ida stroked her hand harder than before. "He's been eager to see you since he heard about you being in the hospital."

"When did he get back into town?"

Ida stopped rubbing Sydney's hand.

"Ida?" Sydney prompted when the other woman didn't answer.

"Not too long ago. You've been so busy you must not have noticed his return. I'm sure once you see him you'll feel better. After all, what woman wouldn't be eager to see her boyfriend?"

Dante took a seat at the head of his dining room table, which was large enough to accommodate all his brothers and their mates. "Thanks for coming everyone. I know you all are busy in your own lives but I felt this was matter of some urgency."

Isis, who sat on his right hand side, took his hand and squeezed it in a show of her support. Dante briefly smiled at his beautiful shifter bloodmate before turning his attention to the rest of the occupants.

"You know there's nothing more important than family." GianMarco smiled at his brother. He looked more relaxed and happy than he had in years. His arm was casually draped around his bloodmate Maggie's shoulder.

Romeo nodded. "I agree with Marco. So what's the emergency? Another rogue threat? Anyone still looking for retaliation because of what we did to The Council of Immortals? I'm not averse to busting some heads. I haven't seen any action in months...well...at least that kind of action." He turned to his bloodmate Christine and gave her a wolfish grin.

Christine popped Romeo on the arm. "Not here. Besides, the kids are in the other room. You better watch it mister or you won't be getting any kind of action."

Romeo threw his hands up in surrender. "Okay, I'll behave."

Christine giggled. "Not too much."

Dante couldn't help but smile indulgently at his family and how well everyone was doing in their lives. He glanced at Niccolo, the quietest of the bunch, who rested his hand possessively on the back of his bloodmate Sasha's neck. Sasha had the self-satisfied smirk on her lips of someone who had just been thoroughly fucked and considering those two had been the last ones to arrive it wasn't hard to deduce that is exactly what had happened.

Despite the happy portrait his family painted, someone was missing. Giovanni.

"No, it isn't anything like that, Romeo," Dante finally answered. "Besides, we all agreed we'd take some time off from Underground business so that we can focus on family for a while. Any rogue threat can be ably handled by my agents for now."

"So what brings us here today?" Romeo asked.

Dante sighed. "It's family related. Lately, I've been having these premonitions that one of you is in trouble. I've had strange reactions, like heat flashes and moments when I can't control my abilities. These instances are very brief but it's enough to cause concern. I felt like one of you was in pain. But as we sit here it's obvious no one at this table is in peril. And Nico, I'm sure you would know if Jagger was in danger."

Niccolo nodded. "Of course. He and Camryn are doing well. I spoke to Jagger just this morning."

Dante's nephew Jagger, who happened to be a hybrid vampire warlock, had recently gone on his mystical journey in Russia under his uncle Steel's tutelage to master his warlock abilities. During this period Camryn his bloodmate was finishing up the last semester of grad school. The two had recently reunited and planned to move closer to the family when Camryn graduated. That was when they would wed, much to Sasha's delight.

Dante nodded his head, pleased that all was well with his nephew and his bloodmate. "That's good to hear. But as I was saying, Isis and I determined that since it was none of us in trouble, it had to be Giovanni."

Everyone around the table went quiet as they looked around at each other.

GianMarco finally broke the silence. "This makes sense now. I didn't mention anything before, because like you Dante, I had checked to make sure everyone of us was okay. I saw no issue so I dismissed it."

Romeo raked his fingers through his short blond hair. "I did as well."

Dante looked toward Nico for confirmation.

"Yes. Me too," Nico said. "Now I feel like a major asshole. How could we have ignored our brother he's in trouble?"

Sasha leaned over and gave Nico a quick hug. "Don't be too hard on yourself. It's a simple mistake. You four have always had each other. You didn't know Giovanni even existed up until some months ago. Giovanni being the one in danger wouldn't naturally occur to you."

"Yes, but we should have known," Nico countered.

"Sasha is right," Dante spoke up. "We were all off. Part of us not having the automatic connection to him as our kind does with our bloodlines is because he's much older than us. He's been able to use his abilities in a way that kept us blocked off from him for centuries. Also, the dark magic he used to practice could have also had something to do with it.   We've never *felt* him before— until now. I feel him like I never have before but what I'm getting from him doesn't make sense. The last time I felt this way was when Marco was going through *la morte dolci.*"

Maybe that's what he's going through. It's quite possible that after all this time he's found his mate," Maggie pointed out.

Dante nodded in agreement. "That could be it but I sense that there's more to it. Something I can't explain. Something dark. We have to find him. I've already put some feelers out to get his whereabouts. As soon as I hear back from my contacts, I think we should go to Giovanni and help him."

"Wait a minute," Sasha spoke up. "I think I might know something. I didn't think anything of it at the time but this could possibly be connected.

"If you remember anything, Sasha, you must tell us," Niccolo prodded gently.

"When I talked to Steel some weeks ago, we talked about a spell he'd used to purge black magic from someone who's practiced it for a while. He'd only ever used it as a counter spell and not on someone who voluntarily wanted to be purged. As you all know, I'm still trying to gain a foothold of my own powers, but my gift enables me to connect with the keepers of spells so ancient they were around before man walked the Earth. He asked me if there's a way to find out if the spell presents any other side effects beyond the ones that are known. I told him of a place where he could access that information. He didn't elaborate on why he needed to know and I didn't think to ask because I figured he had a good reason."

"Do you think Giovanni might have contacted Steel to perform such a spell on him?" Dante asked.

"It's possible. But from what I understand, the spell requires the power of three. The twins or I would be the only ones Steel would trust to take on such a task with him. The twins were recently in Moscow for a visit," Sasha explained.

"Do you think something went wrong with the spell? Could that be the reason why we're starting to feel these weird symptoms?"

Sasha shrugged. "It's possible but I can't know with absolute certainty unless you find Giovanni. I'll attempt to get in contact with Steel and if I can't reach him, I'll try one of the twins. Someone should know something. Excuse me. I'm going to need to concentrate while I mind link with one of my brothers." She pushed her chair back and stood up before vacating the table and leaving the room.

Dante's heart sped up as he thought of Giovanni being in some kind of trouble. His brother had done so much for them even though they didn't know it. They owed it to Giovanni to help him out of any situation he was in. "Hopefully the Romanovs will know something."

"We can only hope," GianMarco agreed with a grim expression on his face.

Just then Jaxson, Romeo and Christine's seven year old son walked into the dining room, his face scrunched up in disgust. "What's the matter, champ?" Romeo asked the little boy.

Jaxson folded his arms over his chest. "Gianna took a dump in her pants and she's stinking up the place. She's killing my nose." He swatted the air for effect.

"Oh, boy. I guess that's my cue to go change her." Maggie pushed herself away from the table and got up.

Jaxson turned his attention to his aunt. "What do you guys feed that baby? Skunk Pie? It's not normal for such a little kid to make such a toxic smell." If nothing else the kid was honest. Dante couldn't help but chuckle at his nephew's antics.

Everyone around burst into laughter at the child's straight forwardness.

Romeo rubbed his son's head.

Despite this brief moment of merriment, Dante knew there was trouble ahead to be dealt with, and he hoped they could handle it before it was too late for Giovanni.

## Chapter Thirteen

Giovanni literally felt like he was going insane. Since he'd left Sydney over a week ago, his symptoms had grown worse. It had been a difficult decision to leave the boarding house but the very fact that his illness had gotten worse told him that he'd made the right decision.

He was feverish to a degree that would kill a mortal man. When he'd chanced a look in a mirror he saw that his eyes were blood red. His incisors wouldn't retract and he had the insatiable thirst for blood and pussy. Blood was one thing, but there was only woman he wanted pussy from. And that was Sydney. After sampling her sweetness Giovanni knew no woman would satisfy him the way she did. That she couldn't remember their night together bothered the fuck out of him, but there was nothing he could do about it until he got his body under control.

He thought about getting in touch with one of his old contacts to look out for Sydney while he was indisposed, but the idea of someone other than him watching her every move made him jealous and angry. He couldn't quite explain it. The rational part of him realized that it would be a good idea just in case this dark force that inhabited that house meant to harm her. Giovanni briefly considered contacting his younger brothers but again vetoed that idea. He didn't feel like he had a right to intrude in their lives. Now that Adonis and his mother were gone, they'd probably forgotten all about him. He couldn't be certain but it was hard to focus on anything at the moment other than wanting to be with Sydney and how much pain he was currently in.

He promised himself that when he was better, he'd go back to her. At least then he'd be in a better position to help her. After he left the hospital he headed back to the house to grab his bag. The only person who'd been in resident was Darlene, much to Giovanni's annoyance.

*Darlene stepped out of her bedroom just as Giovanni walked past her door to get to his room. "Hey there. You going somewhere?" He turned around to see her in nothing but a floor length negligee that covered most of her body but left nothing to the imagination. He could tell she wore nothing beneath the green silk as it skimmed her more than generous curves. She looked as if she was in the mood for entertaining but all Giovanni felt was mild disgust. No doubt she was a beautiful woman but she wasn't for him. The predatory gleam in her jade-colored eyes seemed too desperate and he didn't forget the insults she'd thrown at Sydney. Besides, when it came to women, Giovanni was old-fashioned. He preferred to be the one doing the chasing.*

*He wasn't in the mood to be polite when he needed to be as far away from here as possible. "Yes. To my room. Not that it's any of your business."*

*She raised a dark red brow and her mouth circled in a silent "oh". It was apparent she wasn't used to being talked to in this manner. "Well there's no rush. Why don't you come into my room for that drink? Those two stick-in-the-muds who run this house don't serve alcohol so I have to get my own. Let's say you and I have a little fun?" Darlene ran her finger down the center of his chest, fluttered her eyes and pushed her thin lips into a pout.*

*Even if he had been the least bit turned on by her, his dick would have gone woefully soft by now. He captured her hand*

and squeezed it. "He narrowed his eyes." What on Earth would make you think I was interested in you?"

She gasped. "You're...you're hurting me." She tried to yank her hand out of his grasp but he tightened his grip.

"Maybe I want to hurt you," he growled. He could feel that unbearable heat take over his body and he wanted to bite this woman and drain her.

Darlene began to yank her hand in earnest but the more she fought the more he wanted to cause her pain.

Giovanni released her as his incisors descended. Unable to control himself he slammed Darlene against the wall. She released a blood-curdling scream that only pissed him off. He slapped his palm over her mouth and sunk his teeth into her bare shoulder where he spotted a delicious blue vein.

She fought and squirmed against him as he drank from her. The heady rush of taking this blood in such a savage way fueled the beast that lurked within him.

It didn't matter that Darlene stopped fighting because a vampire's bite was like an aphrodisiac that gave pleasure. All Giovanni could concentrate on was how this blood didn't compare to Sydney's. In fact, the more he drank, the angrier he grew. He pulled away none too gently, not caring enough to extract his teeth from her skin slowly so as not to rip her flesh, which is exactly what he did.

Darlene clutched the wound and looked at him in surprise, shock and horror as blood splattered everywhere.

Seeing her on the ground with her negligee getting darker from the blood dripping down her neck brought Giovanni out of his daze.

Fuck! What had he done? What if this had been Sydney? Lately it felt like all he'd been doing was fucking up. His only explanation for acting out this way was la morte dolci. He seemed to lose control at the most inopportune moments like now and Giovanni wasn't sure how much longer this moment of clarity would last.

*He wanted to leave right away, but if he left Darlene like this, she just might bleed out, however if he didn't leave soon, there was a chance someone could stumble upon this bloody scene and there was no telling how he'd react.*

*Even though he didn't particularly like the woman currently cowering away from him, he didn't want to see her die. He held out his hand to her but she whimpered and scooted away. Not having the patience to coddle her, Giovanni leaned over and scooped her up. She squirmed against him. "No! Don't hurt me. I promise I won't tell anyone. I'll leave this place tonight and go back home. I have a really wealthy father. He'll pay you whatever you want."*

*Giovanni maneuvered her in his arms so that he could open her bedroom door. Then he carried Darlene to her bed. "If your father is so wealthy then what are you doing here?" He didn't ask because he actually cared, he just wanted to distract her from what he was going to do next.*

*"He lowered my allowance and I couldn't stay in my nice apartment by the river. It's all because of that witch he married." Darlene's eyes filled with unshed tears.*

*Giovanni slit his wrist with his sharpened nail, drawing blood. He wasn't sure what this little bit of his blood would do to Darlene while he was in this state but he would rather take his chances than to have her bleed to death. These few drops of his blood shouldn't hurt her, he figured. He yanked her hand away from her shoulder and pressed his opened, wrist against her wound.*

*"What are you doing?" She began to squirm in panic.*

*"Relax. This should take care of your injury. Now sleep." He put all his concentration into that suggestion and thankfully her eyes drifted shut. He kept his wrist against her wound until he saw her skin slowly mend. By the time he pulled away from her, she was nearly healed. The only indication that there*

*had ever been an injury was the dried-up blood coating her nightie, and her neck and shoulder area.*

*He was thankful that his power of suggestion was back although he wasn't sure how strong it was. He leaned over until his lips nearly touched her ear. "After you wake, you will pack your bags and go back home to your father. You will apologize for being a spoiled brat and you'll start talking responsibility for your own life. Go to school or get a job. Become a responsible adult. When you wake up, you won't remember seeing me. I wasn't here."*

*"I won't remember a thing," she whispered in her sleep.*

*"Good girl." Giovanni pulled away from her. When he was certain she wouldn't stir, he hurried to the bathroom and grabbed a towel to clean up the blood in the hallway. Then he returned to Darlene's room and wiped her up the best he could. Her injury was now completely healed. There was still blood on her nightie but that couldn't be helped as he had no intention of going through the trouble of undressing her and finding something else for her to wear. He smeared the bloody towel under her nose. Perhaps when she woke up she'd think she had a bad nosebleed in her sleep.*

*Once he was sure that nothing was out of order, he went back to his room, stuffed the bloody towel into his duffle bag, gathered all of his items and headed out of the house without looking back.*

*He wanted to get away from here before Sydney became his next victim.*

Giovanni bought a ticket on the first train out of town. He must have traveled several hours, fighting the urge to rip the other passengers apart. When he couldn't take the temptation anymore, he found himself in a town two states away from Sydney's. He paid for a room in a seedy motel, the kind that took cash and didn't ask questions. It was heavily populated with miscreants and people on the fringe of society, a place where one went to get lost.

He was in so much pain, he welcomed death. Giovanni lay on the bed, covered in sweat, burning up. He clawed at the sheets, howling in agony. The only thing that gave him a modicum of relief was when he focused on Sydney's beautiful image. More than anything he wanted to go to her and claim her as his but then he remembered what happened with Darlene.

The physical hurt was unlike anything he'd ever endured. Giovanni screamed his misery as another wave of pain hit him. It felt like every bone in his body was breaking and someone was squeezing his heart in their hands.

"How does this feel, brother?"

Giovanni squinted and saw Adonis by his side. His brother's fist had gone through his chest and Adonis had a death grip on Giovanni's heart.

He shook his head. This couldn't be happening. Giovanni squinted. He had to be seeing things.

"Adonis?" he whispered.

"In the flesh."

"But... you're dead. I—"

"You killed me? Yes, I remember that. You took my heart in your hand and crushed it to a pulp."

"I had to do something. You wouldn't have stopped otherwise."

"I did what I had to do to make that man pay for what he did to me, did to us."

"No. It's not what our father did to us, it's what our mother did. She created this mess. Our papa wanted to help us. He would have taken you in with him but you refused."

"And why would I want to live with him and his whore? He seduced our mother and abandoned her."

"You're talking crazy. Maria was a fine woman and you killed her and our father. They didn't deserve it. You would have kept killing unless I did something."

"You chose them over me. You saved them and not me."

"They were vulnerable."

"What about me, Giovanni? Wasn't I vulnerable too?" Suddenly Adonis transformed into his childhood version.

It was official: Giovanni believed he had truly lost his mind.

"Adonis, I tried to reach you. I really did," Giovanni tried to reason.

"Maybe you didn't try hard enough. You could have saved me but you didn't. Now how does it feel now that the tables are turned?"

"I'm sorry. More than you could ever imagine."

"Sorry won't bring me back, *brother*. You didn't save me and now I'm going to make you pay." And with that Adonis squeezed Giovanni's heart, intensifying the pain.

Giovanni screamed until his throat was sore. He closed his eyes and prayed for death but when it didn't come he opened them again, and Adonis was gone.

Had it all been in his mind?

The sudden need for blood was more intense than he could imagine. He slid out of bed with one thing on his mind.

Hunt.

## Chapter Fourteen

"Why don't you play a song for us, Sydney?" Ida asked after dinner which had been a quiet affair. The exchange students had decided to go out with friends instead of eating with everyone else. Darlene was no longer a resident. While Sydney was still in the hospital apparently she'd packed her bags and left without notice. Sydney could honestly say that was one tenant she wouldn't miss. Peter decided to stay with his son for a few days because his daughter-in-law recently had a new baby.

And John was gone.

Maybe it was a coincidence but every time she thought about him, she'd get one of her temporary migraines. She felt there was more she should remember about him but something kept preventing her from even trying.

The only occupants in the house were her Ida and Dylan. Usually Sydney liked these times of quiet. She could concentrate more on her music than running the boarding house. But she couldn't shake the uneasy sensation that something wasn't right. She'd felt this way since she came home from the hospital and she wasn't sure why. Nothing seemed out of place. Dylan was attentive and couldn't seem to do enough for her. Even Ida seemed to be in good spirits.

"Um, sure. Was there anything in particular you wanted me to play?"

"You pick, honey," Ida replied.

"Okay." Sydney attempted to stand but Dylan was by her side. He took her by the arm and pulled Sydney to her feet. "Uh, thanks Dylan I was capable of getting out of the chair myself."

He leaned over and kissed her cheek. "I know you can sweetheart. Can't a guy help out his lady? Besides, I don't want you to tire yourself out."

Sydney barely managed not to flinch when his lips touched her skin. She should have been responsive to her boyfriend's advances but she found no enthusiasm whenever he kissed her. In fact, it was yet another thing that didn't seem right. Maybe she was still suffering from the after effects of what sent her to the hospital. "Dylan, I'm blind, not 102 years old."

Dylan chuckled. "I forget that you're Miss Independent." He released her arm. "Fine, go ahead and play something jazzy." He smacked her on the bottom.

Sydney was tempted to elbow him in the gut for that but she managed to contain herself. She counted her steps as she made her way to the piano and took a seat on the bench. As her fingers made contact with the keys, she breathed a sigh of relief. At least something around here felt familiar. Even though Dylan had requested an upbeat song, Sydney found herself playing a melancholy tune about lost love and longing. She swayed to the music, getting completely immersed in the notes she played.

By the time she finished the song, her cheeks were damp. Tears had fallen unheeded down her face and she didn't know why.

"That was beautiful, Sydney." Ida sounded sincere but there was an edge to her voice that made Sydney wonder what her friend didn't like about the performance.

"Thanks. Dylan, what did you think?" Sydney inquired.

"It was nice. But you know I'm not into that classic shit. Too boring for my taste. Now play something fun like I asked you the first time."

She didn't like his tone and it was on the tip of her tongue to tell him exactly that, but a knock on the door interrupted her mid-thought. Frowning, she stood up. "We weren't expecting guests, were we?"

"I don't think so. But I can answer the door," Ida volunteered.

No, just have a seat and relax. You cooked a delicious meal. Rest your feet."

"I'll escort you to the door." Dylan was at her side.

"Dylan, would you stop treating me like an invalid? I know you're just being helpful but it's driving me crazy. I know this house better than anyone else, including you."

"I'm just trying to help."

"You can help me by not trying to do everything for me. Let me answer the door."

When she made it to the front door she called out, "Who is it?"

"Are you the proprietress of this boarding house? Miss Lewis?"

Anyone who looked up her boarding house in the classifieds could find her name so it didn't bother her that he knew who she was. "Yes. Who'd like to know?"

"Dante Grimaldi. I'm here with my brothers and we're wondering if you could help us locate someone who we believe is currently staying in your house."

Sydney was immediately apprehensive. There was no one in the house with the last name of Grimaldi, and it was rare when visitors came to see the house guests without notice because it was frowned upon. For safety reasons there was a rule that all visitors needed to be cleared with Sydney or Ida before they were allowed into her home.

She heard footsteps approach from behind and knew it was Ida because her steps weren't as heavy as Dylan's.

"Who is it? What do they want?" Ida demanded.

"Someone named Dante Grimaldi. He says he's looking for one of our boarders. Should I open the door?" she whispered so the men on the other side of the door wouldn't hear her.

"I'll see what they want." Ida brushed past Sydney and opened the door. "Yes? What do you want?" She greeted the men without preamble.

There was a pause before any of the men answered. Sydney didn't know how many were out there because Dante had said brothers in the plural.

"Our apologies if we're interrupting your dinner but we just need a minute of your time. We're looking for a man who we believe is one of your boarders."

"Hmph," Ida grunted. "What's his name?"

There was another pause. "John Chandler."

Sydney focused her attention on the direction of the voices. Dante, the one speaking sounded similar to John. "Yes. We know him he was—"

"It's our policy not to allow guests in this house without checking them out first. So maybe you should come back again when you follow proper protocol," Ida interrupted, not giving Sydney a chance to finish.

"Ida!"

"I'm thinking about our safety, girl. We don't know these men."

"Ida is it?" The one called Dante asked.

"Yeah, that's my name."

"Ida, you seem tired. I bet you had an exhausting day. You should probably go get some rest." Dante's words were extremely presumptuous but there was a hypnotic quality to his tone and even Sydney found herself yawning.

"You know what? I'm tired. Think I'll go lie down. Sydney, you handle our guests." And just like that Ida walked away. Sydney heard her friend walk up the stairs.

Sydney opened her mouth in amazement. What the fuck just happened? "H-how did you do that? Ida doesn't take orders from anyone."

"I didn't order her to do anything," Dante argued. "I simply made a suggestion."

"Well whatever you did, it worked. But then again, maybe Ida really was tired. It's hard to read people when you can't see their faces."

"You're blind?" Another masculine voice asked in what sounded like surprise. "Umph! My apologies. I didn't mean to be rude."

Sydney imagined someone must have hit or elbowed the man who'd just spoken. She chuckled in amusement. "No worries. I get that a lot when I don't have my cane with me.

"But still, I shouldn't have worded it liked that. My name is Romeo, by the way."

Sydney raised a brow. "As in the Shakespeare play?"

"Something like that." She could hear the smile in his voice. This one was definitely a charmer.

"I'm sorry, but how many of you are there?" She asked just to be cautious even though she felt no imminent danger. At the very least they didn't make any aggressive move to get inside her house.

"There are four of us," Dante answered. "My brother Romeo who has already introduced himself, my other two brothers GianMarco and Niccolo."

Sydney nodded in their direction. "Nice to meet you. I'm sorry, where are my manners? Why don't you guys come in?" She stepped back, opening the door wider.

"We don't want to intrude."

She shook her head. "Oh, you're not intruding. We've already eaten dinner and we were enjoying some music. Follow me."

She waited until she was sure they were all in before closing the door and heading back to the sitting room. "Who are these men?" Dylan demanded as soon as she stepped into the room. "And where is my grandmother?" He hooked his arm around her waist and possessively pulled her to his side. Sydney squirmed in his hold but the more she tried to put some space between the two of them, Dylan's fingers would dig into her sides. Not wanting to make a scene in front of the guests, she forced herself to remain still.

"Um, why don't you all make yourself comfortable? In the meantime, can I get you fellas something to drink? We have water, fresh-squeezed lemonade and sweet tea."

"Nothing for me, thank you. We don't want to take up too much of your time," a new voice answered which was either GianMarco or Niccolo. She couldn't tell.

"Anyone else?"

"No, thank you," the rest of the men said in turn.

"Then why are you here? We don't get many visitors around these parts, especially fancy ones like you." Dylan's sullen tone made it clear that he resented their presence.

Once again Sydney tried to break free of his hold but this time he actually pinched her. Hard.

Though it had hurt, she gasped more from surprise than pain. What the hell was Dylan's problem and why was he acting this way in front of company? He wasn't being himself. She hoped her guests didn't notice.

"Are you okay, Miss Lewis?" There was a slight edge to Dante's voice which told her that he did see what happened.

"Oh, yes. I'm fine." Sydney hoped her words sounded believable. Thankfully Dylan loosened his grip enough for her to slip out of his hold. Figuring most of the other seats were occupied, sat down at the piano bench. Dylan scooted next to her and placed a hand on her knee. Sydney was extremely embarrassed by his display but she had no choice but to play it off.

"So you didn't tell us what you wanted," Dylan broke the silence first.

"We were telling Miss Lewis that we're looking for someone we think is one of her boarders. I believe he goes by the name of John Chandler."

"You see Sydney, I told you that guy was trouble. Now he has people coming around here looking for him. You men have wasted your time coming here. He's gone and good riddance." Dylan emphasized his words with a snort.

"Do you know where he may have went? We were sure he's still be here. At least this is where we'd traced him," Romeo spoke. Sydney wasn't sure why these men were looking for John but the frustration in her guest's voice was very obvious.

Sydney would have told them what she knew but she was cut off by Dylan.

"We already told you what you need to know. That motherfucker is gone. And that's exactly what you should be. Gone."

"Dylan!" He was really starting to piss Sydney off. When their guests were gone she intended to give him a good ol' Southern cuss out.

"Perhaps Dylan has had a long day and is feeling stressed. I bet he wants to take a walk. Don't you, Dylan?" There it was again, that hypnotic timbre in Dante's voice.

"What the hell are you talking—you know what, I'm feeling stressed. I think I'll take a walk." Dylan leaned over and planted a kiss on Sydney's cheek before vacating the piano bench.

When she heard the front door click behind him, Sydney demanded. "Okay, how the hell did you do that? Are you some kind of hypnotist?"

"You could say that," Dante answered.

"I could say anything but what you're not telling me says more than what you are. What's going on and why do you want to get in contact with John? Is he in some kind of trouble?"

The room was quiet for a moment and she wondered if the men were exchanging secret glances with each other. Finally one of them spoke. "Yes, we believe he's in some kind of trouble and it's imperative we find him. How long would you say that he's been gone?" She didn't recognize the voice of the speaker.

"I'm sorry, but could you tell me who just spoke?"

"My apologies, I'm GianMarco."

"GianMarco," she repeated, testing the name on her tongue. "He's been gone for almost a week. I was in the hospital after some kind of freak occurrence in my body when I last saw him. He came by for a visit and told me he was leaving. He said he may or may not be back but he didn't tell me where he was going."

"Shit," one of the men muttered but she couldn't tell which one.

"Is there anything else you could tell me about his visit?"

"How do I know the four of you aren't trying to cause more trouble for John?"

"Because he's our brother. The last thing we want is to cause him any harm. Please, it's important that you help us. He's dealing with an illness that only we can assist him with and if we don't get to him in time there could be major consequences," Dante replied.

"For whom?"

"For him and anyone who's unfortunate enough to be within eyesight of him."

Sydney frowned. "What kind of illness is it? Is it contagious?"

"No. But it does make people not themselves. Someone going through what he is can get very violent."

Sydney wasn't sure how much she could trust these men but the sincerity in their voices was plain. Her gut instinct rarely let her down before. She sighed. "There's really not that much I can tell you about him besides the fact that he was nice and we got along well. But he seemed really troubled. When he first showed up, he slept for three nights straight. I was very close to calling an ambulance. He woke up screaming bloody murder, something about not being able to save someone. I don't know who he was referring to. He said something odd about not having slept in a long time. I think his words were that he had an extreme case of insomnia. And..." She scrunched her forehead. Sydney felt there was something she needed to remember but the harder she tried to dredge up details her head would hurt. She made another attempt and a sharp pain hit her, leaving Sydney winded. "Oh!" she cried out, clutching her head.

"Miss Lewis? Are you okay?"

She shook her head to clear it from the fog that seemed to fall over her. "I think so."

"Please let me. I have a trick that can get rid of headaches by touching the right pressure points," Romeo offered.

Unlike before, this pain didn't quickly disappear and it felt like it was getting worse. Whatever he could do to make it go away would be welcome. She felt him in front her before he placed strong fingers at her temple.

"Sleep," he whispered.

Slowly she drifted out of consciousness.

## Chapter Fifteen

Dante knew what Romeo was going to do before he did it but it was something that needed to be done. While Sydney seemed forthcoming enough, he had a feeling that there was something she wasn't telling them. It even seemed as if she was trying to remember but couldn't. He definitely got a strange vibe about this house and its residents. He'd felt it the second he stepped over the threshold.

Romeo lifted an unconscious Sydney into his arms and carried her to the couch. GianMarco and Niccolo vacated their spots so Romeo could lie Sydney down. He then placed his fingers at her temples again and closed his eyes. Dante watched as his brother attempted to extract whatever information was locked away in Sydney's mind when Romeo pulled back abruptly.

Romeo's incisors descended as he hissed. "What the fuck!"

Dante jumped to his feet. "What's happened?"

"Someone's been tampering with her mind. I can't get to whatever it is she knows. It actually hurt to get past the blocks that were in place."

"Who do you think has been tampering with her mind?" Niccolo questioned, speaking for the first time since their arrival.

Romeo shook his head. "I don't know but this house feels eerie. There's a dark force here but I couldn't begin to pinpoint where it originates. I'm not that familiar with black magic but it kind of feels like when we were in Adonis's castle but not as strong."

GianMarco nodded. "I got that too. Did you notice something strange about the way Ida and Dylan acted? They seemed pretty hostile toward our presence and were very defensive when we brought up Giovanni's alias. I wonder if Giovanni and Dylan had some kind of confrontation. It would certainly explain why Dylan would have hard feelings toward him."

Dante paced the sitting room. "I don't know but we're not going to get any more answers here. But like you I felt darkness as well. I wish we'd brought Sasha with us. She might be able to tell us more about what was happening."

Though the women had traveled with them, they stayed behind at a nearby hotel, ready to converge if needed. Dante didn't think it would be a good idea for all of them to show up here because such a large group might have intimidated the house's occupants.

Dante pounded his fist in his palm, frustrated that Giovanni wasn't at his last known location. During their family meeting when they'd all agreed to search for their estranged relative, Sasha had managed to reach her brother Steel who had directed her to the twins. It was then she'd learned of his location and that they'd had contact with him. They also found out about the incident between Giovanni and Sydney—an incident she clearly didn't remember.

The woman lying on the couch, oblivious to the world around them, was Giovanni's bloodmate and she was in trouble.

"We need to get her out of this place," Dante declared. "We can keep her at the hotel with our bloodmates. Perhaps Sasha could perform a ritual to help Sydney's memory."

Niccolo frowned. "I'm all for that idea but how do you think she'll react when she comes to? Sydney might not take too kindly to being removed from her home."

"I for one think we can't get her out of here fast enough. Between that shriveled old prune and that asshole, it might be best if she was away from them." Romeo grunted. "I wanted to punch that guy in the face. Did you see what he did to her? There's something unnatural about his relationship with Sydney considering what the twins told Sasha. She's Giovanni's bloodmate and I know if Christine were in trouble, I'd want you three to help her by any means necessary."

Dante nodded. "Then it's settled. She's coming with us." Just then his phone rang. He pulled it out of his pocket and saw that it was Isis. "Yes, *belissima*?"

"Are you near a television?" Dante frowned doing a quick scan around the room. He was sure his bloodmate had a good reason for asking such a random question.

"No. Why?"

"We've found Giovanni. And it's worse than any of us could have ever imagined. Much worse."

<><><><><><>

Giovanni shouldn't have left his room but the tiny walls seemed to be closing in on him. He grew claustrophobic with each passing second. His fever was nearly unbearable and his thirst needed sating. As soon as he was outside, however, he regretted not first stopping by one of his safe houses to get a vehicle. Too much temptation littered the streets. There were a group of scantily clad women on the corner stopping cars and asking if the drivers wanted a date.

A few hooded figures loitered around the parking lot and sidewalks talking on cellphones and making deals. Giovanni licked his lips as he wondered what their blood tasted like, and how long it would take to drain every single drop of the crimson gold flowing in their veins.

As that thought entered his mind, he immediately pushed it away. These urges to kill and maim were becoming more frequent and he wasn't sure how much longer he'd be able to hold them off. He should have gone to a more isolated area, but this illness wasn't exactly conducive to thinking clearly.

Giovanni kept his head down as he walked off the hotel property and down the street. He was stopped abruptly when a woman in a leopard cat suit stepped in front of him. She was extremely skinny, almost to the point of emaciation. He was certain an outfit like hers was designed for a more voluptuous woman with curves. On her it sagged in places where it should have clung. The only thing of note on her body was a pair of large breasts that sat on her bony chest like two rocks. Nothing about them appeared natural.

The woman's skin was sallow and her dirty blonde tresses were so thin he could see her scalp through the hairs. Nicotine stained the tips of her fingers, and the way she shook told him that her body was going through some kind of withdrawal. The look of desperation in her washed-out blue eyes might have made him pity her in other circumstances, but all he could think about was snapping her neck for getting in his way.

"Move," he said with a low growl.

"Do you want, some company, big boy? For twenty dollars I can make you feel so good." She ran her finger down the length of his arm.

"I'm not interested." He attempted to walk around her but she once again halted his progress. "What are you? Some kind of homo?" She seemed incredulous that he could turn down her brand of charms, although in his estimation he'd have to question anyone desperate enough to take this woman up on her offer.

He didn't bother dignifying that stupid question with an answer. Once again he walked around her but she grabbed his arm. "Okay, fifteen. Fifteen and I'll suck your dick like you've never had it before, baby. You know you want this." She smiled to reveal all of her front teeth missing.

Giovanni's stomach turned in revulsion. Now completely out of patience he shoved her away. He didn't put too much force in that movement but apparently he didn't need to because she went flying. She landed so hard, one of her leucite heels flew off.

"You son of a bitch! You're going to be sorry," she screamed, scrambling to her feet.

Giovanni continued walking, desperately trying to block out the sounds that whirled around his head. He could hear and see everything at a much more enhanced level. It was even sharper than it had been before he'd lost his powers, and he couldn't tune everything out.

He wasn't sure how much longer he walked before someone yelled, "Hey, man!"

Giovanni ignored it because there were other people on the street the person could have been calling to. He doubted the person was talking to him until he felt a hand aggressively grasp his shoulder. "I was talking to you, fool."

Giovanni spun around so fast that it must have surprised the man who had grabbed him. "What?" he roared. By now his incisors had dropped and by the heat he felt in his eyes he knew they were bright red.

"Man! What the fuck? This ain't Halloween." A tall dark-skinned man glared at him. "I don't care what the fuck you are. You don't fucking touch one of my girls unless you're paying or want some problems. So you can either compensate me now for manhandling my bitch or I'm going to take it out on your ass." The man reached into his pocket and pulled out a small handgun.

Rage tore through Giovanni. This bottom feeder had the nerve to threaten him and thought he could live to tell about it?

*Do it. Kill him. Give into the darkness.* The voice that floated through his head was Adonis's.

And then Giovanni saw him. Standing behind the pimp was a Adonis smiling. His eyes were glowing and he looked on eagerly. Giovanni blinked and he was gone.

"Do you fucking hear me, man?" his aggressor interrupted Giovanni's thoughts. "Pay me my money."

"Get the fuck away from me," Giovanni roared and before the pimp could react, he grabbed the arm holding the pistol and ripped it clear off the man's body.

The pimp screamed in shock and horror as he fell to the ground clutching the gaping hole where his arm had been.

"I told you to leave me alone," Giovanni punctuated his words with a swift kick to the man's ribs which produced a loud cracking sound.

Around him he vaguely heard the sound of screams. He turned away from the bleeding man and continued his walk, uncaring of the state he'd left his attacker in. Giovanni didn't know how far he got before a loud siren got closer. A horn blared and a magnified voice yelled out to him.

"Freeze!"

Ignoring the command, he kept going.

"I said freeze!"

Once again he disregarded the order.

Suddenly the car sped up and swerved onto the sidewalk directly in front of him. Blocking his progress.

"You're under arrest for disobeying a lawful command," a uniformed officer yelled slamming his car door into Giovanni's stomach as he slid out of the car. A hit like that would have winded an ordinary man but Giovanni barely flinched. The officer seemed to be caught off guard by his lack of reaction but he quickly reached for a device on the side of his belt and aimed it at Giovanni. He advanced on the officer and was met by several bolts of electricity. He shook and roared but remained on his feet. The little bit of self-control he'd been holding on to was gone. He grabbed the officer, lifted him off his feet and tossed him across the street.

Another officer ran toward him, gun drawn. Before Giovanni could react, several bullets plowed into his chest. The sting of the metal ripping through his flesh was painful but it wasn't enough to stop him. When the officer saw that the gun had no effect, he turned to run. "Officer down. We need backup on 57th and West," he yelled into the walkie-talkie on his shoulder. Even as the policemen attempted to slide back into his car, Giovanni grabbed the door and ripped it off its hinges.

He yanked the officer out of the car and sunk his teeth into the side of his neck. The man screamed and yelled. "I have a family!" He cried. This didn't matter to Giovanni because the beast within him needed to be satisfied.

More sirens blasted but he drank thirstily from the flailing officer whose heartbeat grew weaker by the second. More shots rang out and bullets rained into his back and neck. He released the bloodied officer with an agonizing yell. He turned to see several officers surrounding him with guns drawn. He flashed to the closest one and delivered a blow so powerful it caved the side of his face in.

More shots pelted him and he went to his knees as the pain became too great to ignore, not to mention he was fast losing blood which sapped some of his strength.

He looked around him and in the midst of the chaos he saw Adonis with a smirk on his face, clapping at the destruction Giovanni had wrought. "Leave me alone!" He screamed, springing back to his feet. Some officers had since retreated as they witnessed his supernatural strength. A few valiantly attempted to take him down with pepper spray and night sticks. Though these items slowed him down temporarily, it didn't stop him. He gripped an officer in each hand and propelled them together, making their heads crack. They crumpled to the ground.

All he saw was red as he was tackled to the ground by a big brute. The officer rained blows with his stick on Giovanni's head. Even in his weakened state the policeman was no match for him. He wiggled from beneath his attacker and flipped the officer over. He then clawed into the man's cheek and ripping off half his face. The policeman screamed in agony. Giovanni would have eaten his flesh if he didn't catch something out the corner of his eye. He saw his Papa. Standing next to him was a beautiful ethereal blonde. Maria.

They looked on at him with sadness in their eyes. In that moment of clarity, he looked around to see what he'd done. Several officers lay bloodied and injured, some he couldn't tell for certain if they were still alive.

What had he done? He looked toward his papa and Maria. They were gone.

Two large black trucks appeared on the street with the word SWAT in big white letters. Not wanting to hurt anyone else, Giovanni wobbled to his feet, he ran knowing that when he picked up speed, they wouldn't be able to catch him. He kept going and going and had no intention of stopping.

All the while he was running, he thought of Sydney, thankful that he'd gotten far away from her.

## Chapter Sixteen

Sydney buried herself deeper into the softness of the large down comforter. It was so soft and fluffy. The warmth cocooned her, making Sydney not want to move an inch. "Mmm." She rolled over and rubbed her cheek against a pillow so soft, her head sunk in it. Was she in heaven?

As she slowly opened her eyes, she ran her fingers along the bedding and froze. This wasn't her bed. It was too large, too soft. And the sound of cool air generating around her was another indicator that not only was she not in her room but she wasn't in her house. She didn't have central air.

"Where am I?" she whispered more to herself than to anyone who might hear her. The last time she woke up in an unfamiliar place it had been the hospital but there was no hospital that she knew of with bedding that felt quite this expensive. This comforter and sheet reminded her of the time her father had splurged for a night at a nice hotel during a family vacation.

"Ah, so you're finally awake." The voice belonged to a woman. It was warm, and immediately put Sydney at ease when she should have been apprehensive. But still she was in a strange place with a woman she didn't know.

"Wh-who are you?"

"I'm Maggie Grimaldi and you're Sydney, right?"

"Are you John's sister? He only mentioned brothers."

Maggie laughed. "John? Oh, no. I'm GianMarco's wife."

"So you're his sister-in-law?"

"Yes."

"Where am I and why am I here? The last thing I remember is being at home. Your husband and brothers-in-law came by looking for John. I really couldn't give them that much information. I got a headache and Romeo offered to do some kind of trick to take it away. And now I'm here. How?"

"They brought you here. Before you grow alarmed, they did it because they thought you might be in some kind of danger."

Sydney shook her head, scooting away from this woman. Even if what she said was true, they had basically kidnapped her. She didn't know these people or even if John wanted to be found by them. There had to be a reason they were estranged. Right?

"They said John was in some kind of danger. That he's suffering from some kind of illness that makes him a danger to himself and others." The breath hitched in her throat when she remembered what Dante had done. "Dante is some kind of hypnotist. He persuaded my friends to do something out of character. It seemed so weird. A lot of strange things have been happening to me lately and I can't make heads or tails of it."

"I understand you probably have a lot of questions and they deserve to be answered. Just know that everything Dante and the rest of the guys told you is all true."

"They didn't really tell me much."

The bed depressed under Maggie's weight. "There really wasn't much time. It was important to get you out of your house. Like I said, there's some kind of danger. They all felt it."

"Felt it? What are you talking about? Are they a bunch of psychics or something? I've lived in that house for the last eight years with no incident. The only danger I've ever experienced was being kidnapped by four strange men who claim to be related to one of my former boarders. I notice you're being evasive so I doubt asking you anything will yield me any answers."

Maggie placed her hand on top of Sydney's but she immediately snatched it away. "Don't touch me."

Maggie sighed. "I'm sorry. My family is so touchy-feely that I forget myself sometimes."

"It's not that I don't like to be touched, it's just that I don't know you. Your husband and his brothers kidnapped me."

"You weren't kidnapped, Sydney. You were taken out of that house for your own safety."

"And I felt perfectly safe before I met you people. But if I haven't been kidnapped as you say, then I'm free to go?" Sydney threw off her covers and slid out of bed, thankful that whoever tucked her in had left her clothes on. Once she was on her feet she placed her hands out in front of her and took small steps. "I don't suppose one of my kidnappers, oh excuse me, 'rescuers' were decent enough to bring my cane along?"

"It's by the door along with your shoes," Maggie said quietly. "If you really want to go, I can't stop you, and I won't, but seeing as how you don't know where you are, how do you plan to get home? One can only assume you don't drive and you need money for public transportation."

"Well, I hope you'll be decent enough to tell me where we are."

"We're at the Grand Marine, about twenty-five minutes away from your house."

So they were one town over. It wasn't too far from her doctor's office so had a good idea where she was. If she had to rely on the kindness of strangers to get home that's what she'd do. One thing about being blind was that people went out of their way to help her. All she'd have to do was ask for some change and find a bus stop.

Sydney kept going until she felt a sharp pain in her knee. "Shit."

"There's a coffee table there. To your left is a love seat. The bedroom door is about ten paces to your left. When you leave this room you'll be in the main part of the suite. About twenty steps from there is the exit. But I'd rather you didn't go. Don't you want to find out what's wrong with you? Why you're having headaches whenever you try to remember things?"

Sydney stopped mid-step. "How did you know?"

"There's nothing my family keeps from each other. We share things. When the men brought you back they explained what happened at your house."

"Yes, but that doesn't explain how they'd know about the headaches. No one knows about them. I haven't told a soul. I didn't even mention it to a doctor since I left the hospital and honestly I'm not sure why I didn't."

"There are other ways of finding things out."

A chill moved up Sydney's spine. "This is getting too weird. First the hypnotizing thing and now this. It's like someone read my mind."

"In a way, yes they did. You just mentioned not knowing why you didn't tell the doctor about the headaches. Have you thought that maybe something or someone is mentally manipulating you?"

"That's just crazy talk."

"Yet you've witnessed for yourself what Dante could do. Sydney, the world is bigger than you know. There are most that just humans and animals that walk the Earth."

Sydney laughed nervously. "What is this? I feel like I'm on some kind of prank show."

"Trust me when I say I reacted similarly to you when someone first told me there were supernatural beings walking among us; most of them blend in with the rest of the world so you never quite know who is who."

"I don't believe you," Sydney whispered. This woman had to be two pennies short of a dollar. "And even if I did, why are you telling me this?"

"Because you're important to our family."

Sydney shook her head in denial. "I don't know your family. We only met today remember?"

"It's because you're important to Giovanni which makes you important to us."

"Who's Giovanni?" The more Maggie talked, the more confused Sydney became.

"I'm sorry, you know him as John."

"Wait a minute. Are you saying John was using an alias? That can't be. I use an agency that does a background check on any potential boarders. Everything came back normal, John Chandler born in Willingboro, NJ, in 1981."

"Your agency saw what he wanted them to see. I'm probably doing a horrible job at explaining things so maybe you should take a listen to this."

"Listen to what?"

"Give me a second, I need to pull it up on my phone. There's story on the news that might be of some interest to you. There's video footage that appeared in this news clip but the audio should be able to tell you a little bit of what's happening. Now this might not make any sense at first, but I'll explain it to you if you have any questions afterward. I'm going to start playing it now."

"Okay," Sydney agreed cautiously.

There was silence for a moment and then what sounded like a newscast began. *In local news tonight, several police officers have been injured in what's been called one of the most horrific acts of violence in history. In this bystander's video, you see a man attacking officers after taking several bullets to the chest and back in what seems like an act of supernatural strength. Experts believe the man perpetrating the crime was possibly wearing a bulletproof vest and was on a substance call Alligator. Alligator is a new designer drug that has been said to cause irrational violence and erratic behavior. The suspect, described as a white male with black hair, and stands about six foot four, managed to escape. If you see this suspect please do not engage. He is said to be dangerous so please call the police immediately.*

"That's it," Maggie said.

Sydney covered her mouth. That was definitely John's description but was that really him? She couldn't imagine him harming anyone let alone several police officers. "Oh, my God. Tell me what was actually shown in the video."

"It was of Giovanni attacking the cops while they shot him several times. But unlike the news report stated, he was neither on drugs nor wearing a bulletproof vest, and even if he was, don't you think one of those cops would have been a good enough shot to get him in the head at least once? There's no way anyone could survive that many hits and still escape."

Sydney took a step backward and found herself against a wall. "What is he?"

"He's a vampire. We're all vampires…well except for Niccolo and Dante. They're a wit—"

"No," Sydney interrupted the obviously delusional woman. "This can't be real. What you're telling me isn't possible."

"Okay, how about I tell you something about yourself that no one else knows?."

"I seriously doubt you could but you can try."

"Okay. Give me a minute. I'm a relatively new vampire so my mind-reading skills aren't as strong as my husband's, who happens to be over six hundred years old."

Yep. It was official. She was being pranked. "Look, this joke has gone on far enough. I'm leav—"

"You had a sister named Tara."

Sydney rolled her eyes. "Anyone could have looked that information up."

"When she was younger she used to get sick a lot. And you were jealous because she got all the attention. So you hid her favorite doll. But you'd hid it so well you were never able to find it. When she was hospitalized, you were so guilty about hiding that doll you blamed yourself for her hospitalization. You broke your piggy bank, Mr. Pennyworth, and spent the money on a new doll. It wasn't as nice as the one you'd lost but Tara loved it all the same. You couldn't do any wrong in her eyes because you were her big sister and she thought the sun rose and set on you."

By the time Maggie finished talking tears rolled down Sydney's cheeks. She'd forgotten all about the Miss Pretty Tessy incident. That story reminded her of how much she missed Tara. Unlike most sisters the two had rarely argued. They were best friends. Wherever Sydney went, Tara was sure to follow. "My parents didn't even know. They thought I was just being nice when I bought Tara that doll. I didn't have the guts to tell them the truth. And the thing is, I think Tara knew what I did, but she didn't rat me out. She was just that kind of person. I just wish...sometimes I feel that she should have lived instead of me." She hastily wiped the tears away.

"You were a child. We all do impulsive, selfish things when we're young. The fact that you tried to atone for what you did shows that you're not a bad person."

"You really are a vampire, aren't you?" Sydney whispered.

Maggie chuckled. "That's pretty wild, isn't it? Nearly two years ago, I was just a regular human like you. I'd recently separated from this toad of a man and I was just getting back on my feet. That's when I met GianMarco. Trust me, I was just as skeptical as you were."

"But he turned you?"

"Yes. He did it because I was pregnant with his child. The baby, being a vampire, would have drained a human vessel."

"Vampires can procreate? I thought they were dead."

Maggie sighed. "You have a lot to learn Sydney, and I promise I'll get you up to speed, but I think you should meet the other ladies."

"Other ladies?"

"My sisters-in-law."

"And they're all vampires as well?"

"Christine is, who is Romeo's bloodmate . Bloodmate is what vampires call their lifelong partners, by the way. Sasha, Niccolo's bloodmate, and Isis, Dante's bloodmate, are not."

"They're human?"

"No. Sasha is a witch and Isis is a shifter but you're probably more familiar with the term werewolf, although

I wouldn't use that word around her. Shifters are very sensitive about that word. It's almost as bad as if you called me or you the N-bomb."

"Oh. You're black like me?" Sydney didn't know why she pictured all vampires to be pale creatures, gothic-looking beings.

"Yes. We come in all different ethnicities and cultures. Christine is Asian, Sasha is Russian and Isis is a mixture of Dominican and Bengali. So we're our own rainbow coalition."

"Wow, this is a lot to take in."

"It's understandable."

"So John, I mean Giovanni, is a vampire as well?"

"Yes."

"But he's ill, you say? It's possible for vampires to get sick?"

"Not normally but this is a condition only vampires are susceptible to. Which brings us to why you're here. When the men were at your house, we saw that news report and contacted Dante. Giovanni is in the crazed throes of what we call *la morte dolci*. It's really hard to explain, but the abbreviated version of it is a vampire suffers from this illness when they are denied what they require most. We believe that something is you."

Sydney placed her hand against her heart with a gasp. "Why me?"

"Because we believe you're his bloodmate."

## Chapter Seventeen

Nya tossed and turned in bed. She hadn't had a decent night's sleep since she came to her hideaway. For the last couple centuries she'd lived with a madman, yet she had still cared about him even though she had never admitted it until recently. Adonis had not only been her maker, taking her away from a bleak existence, he was also her bloodmate.

It was hard to give her love to someone who killed innocents but she'd loved him all the same, much to her secret shame. But even as she loved him, she'd hated him too, hated what he was, and his actions. She hated that he'd turned her into the monster that she was now. She'd never asked for immortality and he'd stolen that choice from her. For that she didn't think she'd ever forgive him. It was a curse seeing people she cared about grow old and die around her while she stopped aging at thirty-five.

Her only connection to humanity had been finding the child that had been ripped from her arms when she was just sixteen. She'd followed that child, a boy as he grew into a young man, watched out for him as he started a family of his own, three children, a boy and two girls. She watched as those children had children and so forth.

Nya's interest in her descendants, however, seemed to anger an already crazed Adonis, who was jealous and possessive on a good day. But on a bad day there was no reasoning with him. In a fit of rage, he'd wiped out nearly every single one of her progeny, claiming they took Nya's time and attention away from him. Devastated, she decided to keep her distance from the remaining survivors, which happened to be a family with two children. The parents eventually grew old and died, while one of their offspring, a girl, tragically died as a child due to a severe allergic reaction. The boy had eventually grown up, married and had two daughters. Their names were Sydney and Tara, the last two in her line.

Whenever she was stateside, she always made an effort to visit though she never approached, just observed, wondering what her life could have been if she'd been allowed to just be. Of course when she was human times had been different, but at least she wouldn't have been bound to a maniac. Ten years ago, she'd made one of her trips to the family's little town to find out that they had been in a tragic accident that had taken the lives of the husband, wife and one daughter. Sydney, who had been left blind, was her last connection to humanity. It almost became an obsession with her to keep Sydney safe. On one of her last trips Nya dared to do something she never had the nerve to do. She'd introduced herself to Sydney in the guise of someone who was selling magazine subscriptions.

Just to be in Sydney's presence had filled Nya with sadness. She had no right to intrude into this woman's life. And as much as it pained her, she knew then that she had to stay away, because she didn't want Adonis to harm Sydney, but mainly because it was just too painful to be reminded of all that she'd been robbed of. It was then she had enlisted Giovanni's aid because he was one of the few people she could trust.

It was important for her to keep that connection even if she couldn't do it herself. Besides, when she'd actually met Sydney, Nya couldn't help feeling that there was something very wrong even though the young lady herself seemed fine. She just couldn't shake this premonition of impending doom. It was the same feeling she had at this very moment.

Frustrated, she rolled out of bed and grabbed her phone. As was her habit, she scrolled through her newsfeed to find out what was going on in the world. One story had her immediately clicking on the thumbnail. *Terror on the Streets* was the title of the video that was attached with the story. She watched in horror as the grainy video showed a man brutalizing several police officers. Though the film didn't show the perpetrators face clearly, she could make out just enough of him to know exactly who it was. Her stomach fell to her feet.

This was not the Giovanni she knew. From the looks of it he'd gone rogue but she was sure there was a pretty good reason why and for that she had to help him. Even though it was her intention to stay in this little villa off the coast of Mexico for a few more months, she realized it was time to come out of hiding. It didn't matter that she was being tracked by a pair of warlocks on a mission, or that she wanted to shut herself off from other people. Her friend was in trouble and she would be there for him as he had been there for her. She only hoped Sydney hadn't been hurt in the melee.

Dante breathed a sigh of relief as he stepped out of the hospital. He believed he'd gotten all of them. After seeing that video plastered all over the media he and his brothers had gone into damage control mode. One of the many tasks performed by his Underground was clean-up when an immortal showed their powers around humans. Memories had to be wiped out, and plausible explanations given to put people's minds at rest. He'd done it several times when rogues got out of control. He never thought he'd had to do it for one of his brothers.

As soon as they'd seen that insane video of Giovanni going berserk, they'd hurried to that area as quickly as possible. Each one of them had been assigned with a task. Dante had put Niccolo in charge of searching for Giovanni, while it was up to GianMarco to sway the news outlets into believing the video had been a hoax. Romeo's job was to find any and all witnesses to the actual incident and wipe their memories of it. And Dante's assignment was to make sure none of the police officers remembered what happened, which meant he had to take care of several hospital staffers and paramedics as well. Dante also administered a little of his blood to each of the officers who had been severely injured. With his blood they would heal quickly with no ill effects.

There was only one casualty in the whole matter. A Lamar Smith, also known as Smooth Money as Dante had learned. He'd bled out by the time the paramedics had reached him. He'd been convicted of trafficking, kidnapping, assault, and racketeering. From what Dante had determined from getting into the police database, Lamar had only been out on the street because his lawyer had gotten him out on a technicality. He was known for taking underage girls and forcing them into prostitution.

While it would have been best had no lives been lost, there was no doubt the man was a scumbag. Dante was at least thankful no one else had died from Giovanni's tirade.

Of course the mission presented to them had been huge which is why Dante had contacted some of his agents who could get to the area easily. Thankfully Sasha had contacted her brothers who were also on their way. With their magic, they would be able to take care of any property damage, like the whole thing had never happened.

With a sigh he slipped into his rental car, exhausted from the tasks he'd spent the better part of the day accomplishing. He wondered how the women faired with Sydney. Grabbing his phone he punched in Isis's name.

She answered on the first ring. "Dante! I miss you," she greeted.

A warmth spread throughout him at the sound of her voice. It didn't matter that they hadn't been away from each other a full day, whenever she wasn't near it felt like a piece of him was missing. "I miss you too, *bellissima*. How are things going with you?"

"I should be asking you that question, but things are going well on my end. Sydney is awake. The girls and I have just spent the better part of three hours explaining the supernatural world to her. I think she's still a little confused but at least she finally believes us, although it took some convincing. I shifted and let her pet me while I was in wolf form and then Sasha levitated her. I think that really freaked Sydney out. She may still have questions about Giovanni, like why he was using an alias, but we explained to her that it was something he'd have to tell her himself. She said she's willing to listen when they get a chance to talk."

"That's good to hear. I had a good feeling about her when we met. She seems very nice. I don't think she'll have a problem fitting in with our clan at all. Giovanni's a lucky man."

"Speaking of Giovanni, what's the situation down there? I noticed the video is no longer available online. In fact it looks like it's been scrubbed from the entire Internet."

"Yes, GianMarco convinced the news outlet that the video was a hoax. I employed a team of hackers to have it removed from any and all sites. Even if people believed Giovanni was just a regular man on drugs, there would be others with questions who might come looking for our kind. It could have put us in a precarious situation."

"Was the originator of the video found?"

"Yes, Romeo located him and confiscated the man's phone and computers. Those videos can sometimes be found in someone's cloud storage and we didn't want to take that chance."

"Good idea. What about Giovanni? How close are you guys to locating him?"

"That I'm not sure of." Just as he finished that statement, his phone beeped indicating that another call was coming through. Dante frowned as he looked at the screen to see who it was before putting the phone back to ear. "I just might have my answer in a minute. Niccolo is calling in. I'm sorry, but I have to go."

"I understand. I love you."

"I love you too, *bellissima*. Take care." He clicked over to take his brother's call. "Niccolo, tell me you've found him."

"I believe I have. He's about an hour away from where everything happened. Giovanni is holed up in an industrial section with a lot of abandoned buildings. He's hiding in one of them and we can hear his screams of pain. He keeps calling out Adonis's name. We have agents posted around the area to discourage anyone from coming close so we're keeping a lookout to make sure he doesn't wander off again."

"Okay. Did you contact the others?"

"Not yet. You were my first call but I'm on it now. I'll contact the twins as well."

"Good thinking, Nico. There's strength in numbers. Give me your exact address and I'll be there as soon as I can."

Niccolo rattled off the address. "I'm hanging up now. I'll call you back if anything changes."

"Sounds good."

Dante clicked off the phone, hoping they would reach Giovanni before he could cause anymore destruction.

"I still can't believe this is happening. I feel like I'm going to wake up and this will all be a really strange dream," Sydney mused aloud. She could barely finish the food on her plate because there were still so many questions she needed answered. Though she'd wanted to deny the existence of immortal beings and the supernatural, there was no doubt what she herself had experienced.

How else could Maggie and Christine pull things from her mind that no one else would know? And then there was Isis. Though Sydney couldn't visually see the transformation, she could hear the snapping of bones and moving of internal organs as Isis had morphed into a large furry animal. In wolf form Isis's head was level with Sydney's chest. She'd felt the wolf's muzzle, and stroked her back, and ran her fingers along its tail. And when Sasha made her float through the air as if she was just a feather, there was no denying anything these women had told her.

She'd had question upon question, to which each of the women had answered patiently. After what seemed like hours, Christine suggested they get something to eat, which is how they'd ended up in the hotel's restaurant.

"Believe, it Sydney." Christine who sat to her right, patted her on the hand.

"This is all going to take some getting used to. I still don't understand how I could possibly help Giovanni. I mean, if he's in this *la morte dolci* as you've explained, how can I bring him out of this illness? I heard the video and know what he's capable of. What if he…"

"He would never hurt you. At least not intentionally," Isis answered.

Sydney snorted. "The way you worded that doesn't exactly inspire confidence."

"I think what Isis is trying to say is that the last thing Giovanni would want is to hurt you. You're special to him. Sometimes when a vampire is in the throes of this madness they can hurt others around them, including the ones they care about, but it's never a conscious thing," Sasha explained. "That is why he'll have his family around him to make sure no harm comes to you."

Sydney moistened her now dry lips with the tip of her tongue. "But what do I need to do exactly?"

Christine squeezed Sydney's hand. "Just be there for him. When you two are together you'll know what to do. Trust us."

"You make it sound so simple when I barely know this man. I've only had a couple conversations with him and now you guys are saying I'm his bloodmate, the one meant to be with him for eternity." That was the part Sydney had the most trouble with. How could she be this man's heart's desire when they barely knew each other? Although Sydney felt that there was something she ought to remember, her head ached whenever she tried.

"But ask yourself this: those couple of times you were around him, you felt this unexplainable pull toward him, didn't you?" Maggie asked.

"I...yes," she whispered. "I did. I felt safe with him. And we shared a kiss that was like nothing I'd ever experienced. It was so powerful, so full of...I don't exactly know how to explain it. I instantly felt connected to him. It's seems like I've known him all my life and that there's so much more to this but my mind has been cloudy lately."

"Sydney," Sasha began, "there's something else I've been meaning to talk to you about, but since you've brought it up I think its best that we discuss it now."

Sydney shuffled in her seat. "That sound ominous."

"Well, we mentioned earlier that the men removed you from your house because they felt some dark force. They believed that you were in some kind of danger. I've observed you and notice there's an aura about you that isn't quite right. I believe this memory loss you've suffered is unnatural. Someone has been tampering with your mind."

Sydney frowned. "How can that be? I've only had these memory lapses recently. It could be related to my hospitalization."

"No. I think it's more than that, and if you would allow me I can see if I can unlock those memories that are hidden away," Sasha offered.

"I don't know. The last time someone offered to help me with my head, I blacked out and ended up in this hotel."

"Please, trust us. We'd never do anything to harm you, Sydney," Isis assured her.

"I have to think about this." Sydney sighed. "I'm sorry, but I need to go to the restroom."

"Would you like one of us to go with you?" Maggie asked.

"No, thank you. I have my cane. I'm sure I'll manage just fine. Just point me in the direction I need to go."

"You'll actually have to exit the restaurant and turn left into the lobby. The women's restroom should be the first door on your right," Maggie directed.

"Thank you."

The restroom was right where Maggie said it would be. Once she had relieved herself and washed her hands she headed out the door only to bump into someone. "Oh! I'm so sorry."

"Sydney! I'm so glad I found you. We have to get out of here now. There are some really bad people out there."

"Ida? What are you doing here?"

"It doesn't matter. I'm here to take you away from here. Dylan has been worried sick about you. I have too. Come on child." Ida took Sydney's hand.

Part of her wanted to resist but then she realized there was absolutely no reason why she was here in the first place. She didn't even remember how she'd ended up in this hotel. "Okay. Let's go. Back to Dylan."

## Chapter Eighteen

Dante stepped cautiously into the building, worried about what he might find. Thankfully, by the time he'd joined the rest of his brothers he learned that Giovanni was still in the same location. Giovanni's howls and screams of agony could be heard before he even got out of his vehicle. There was so much pain and suffering in those cries that it tore at Dante's heart. It made Dante realize just how much Giovanni must have suffered throughout the years.

Romeo, GianMarco, Niccolo and the twins followed closely behind him. He'd ordered the other agents keep lookout at their posts outside. The old warehouse smelled of oil and dust. It took a moment for Dante's eyes to adjust to the darkness but once it did he continued on, following the sound of Giovanni's voice. He halted as something scurried across his shoes. He looked down to see a rat the size of a small house cat. He scrunched his nose in disgust. "Be cautious, men. There are large vermin everywhere."

"I can do a quick spell to light this place up," Blade offered

Dante shook his head. "We don't want to alarm Giovanni. There's no telling what will set him off in this state. Let's go."

They came to a metal stairwell. "Sounds like he's upstairs," GianMarco observed.

Once they got closer to the source of the noise, Dante could feel his brother's presence getting stronger. Giovanni's pain was almost tangible. Dante winced from the physical response he had towards his brother's agony. Though he wanted to run to Giovanni and offer comfort, he continued to step cautiously.

Finally when it felt like they'd traversed the entire length of the warehouse they found him. Sitting in a corner mumbling to himself was Giovanni. Dante hadn't been sure what to expect but seeing his brother in this state had certainly not been it. Giovanni was still covered in blood from head to toe. His hair was a mess and his clothing was torn. His incisors were visible and his fingers were pointed claws which he used to gouge his arms in some barbaric form of self-mutilation. Every time he would tear his flesh open he'd let out an agonizing scream. Then he'd give his face the same treatment, ripping chunks off of himself and not giving his body the proper chance to heal.

"I'm so sorry, Adonis," he whispered. He clawed his face again, tearing off more flesh, and while he did this, he released another agonizing scream.

"Giovanni," Dante softly whispered his brother's name. He couldn't stand seeing Giovanni torture himself this way. He could only imagine the kind of guilt the older vampire must be feeling to harm himself in that way. It was then he realized that while a bloodmate was vital to a vampire's existence, the thing had drove Giovanni's madness was the remorse he felt over Adonis.

With a growl, Giovanni raised his head. He jumped to his feet with lightning speed and charged toward them. Unlike Giovanni's previous victims however, Dante and his crew were prepared.

One of the twins must have uttered a quick spell because the lights suddenly illuminated the room. The abrupt change in atmosphere must have temporarily distracted Giovanni because it enabled Dante to duck away from the blow that Giovanni sent his way. He quickly moved behind Giovanni and placed him into a full nelson. He was strong but Giovanni was older and now that he was currently in the throes of *la morte dolci* he was even stronger.

Giovanni wiggled out of his hold and tossed Dante across the room. "Get away from me," the older vampire roared.

Romeo and GianMarco rushed toward Giovanni and each one them grabbed an arm.

"Now would be a good time to perform some kind of spell to stabilize him," Niccolo suggested to the warlocks.

The twins seemed to already be on it. They joined hands and began to chant.

"Any day now," Romeo yelled as he struggled to hold on to Giovanni.

"These things take time, Ro." Niccolo joined GianMarco and Romeo in trying to restrain Giovanni.

Without warning, Giovanni went stiff.

"You can let him go now," Cutter advised.

"Are you sure?" Dante asked.

Blade nodded. "Let him go and find out for yourselves."

They all stepped away from Giovanni who still remained in the exact position. His eyes were blood red and he looked pissed. "Let me go!" he roared.

"No." Dante shook his head. "We want to help you."

"You can help me by fucking off. You don't care about me. You didn't care about Adonis. You wanted him dead and you were glad to see him gone." Giovanni seemed to strain against the invisible force that kept him immobile. The veins in his neck began to throb and they looked as if they would explode.

Dante closed his eyes against the pain in those words. He released a long, heavy sigh. "I don't deny that I wanted Adonis dead but that's because he did a lot of evil things. Maybe the circumstances would have been different had we known he was our brother. We would have tried a different tactic. But we didn't know and did what we thought was the right thing. Had we not gone after Adonis, he would have continued to wreak havoc in our lives. Adonis tortured us, killed our allies, and took our mother and father. He murdered an innocent baby in the name of revenge against a man who had no ill will toward him. He was evil and needed to be stopped."

"Stop saying that!" Giovanni's eyes grew large in his rage. He snarled at them, showing off his sharp incisiors. Though his ripped skin had started to heal, Giovani still made a frightening sight. "None of you knew him like I did. You didn't hold him in your arms as he breathed his last breath. You silently cheered as our brother died. Had I not been there you probably would have kicked him when he was down."

Dante shook his head in denial. "That's not true. No one took pleasure in seeing him die. Yes, I'm not sorry that he's gone because his death was necessary. But more than anything, I was saddened because I knew how much he meant to you. At some point in his life, he must have been a different person, and I'm sorry I didn't know that Adonis instead of the one he showed to us."

"Lies! Don't pretend like you fucking care!" Giovanni yelled. Though his head remained still, he turned his red-eyed stare toward the twins. "Set me free, warlocks!"

Cutter smirked. "Not until you've calmed down."

Giovanni growled. "Fuck all of you! When I get out of this, I will kill you all!"

"You don't know what you're saying, Giovanni. That's the sickness talking. You wouldn't have spent the last few centuries looking over us only to kill us," Niccolo reasoned.

For the first time since they'd confronted him, Giovanni looked uncertain but then he snarled mutinously. "Maybe if I would have let Adonis kill you then he'd still be alive."

Dante stepped forward and placed his hand on Giovanni's shoulder. "Well I'm glad you didn't because then we wouldn't have gotten this chance to know you. Whether you believe it or not we care about you and want you to be happy."

"Lies. You don't care. You want to destroy me! Adonis says so!" Giovanni screamed.

"Adonis is dead," Romeo pointed out.

"No he's not! He's right behind you!"

Dante turned around and frowned before turning back to his brother. "Giovanni...there's no one there."

Was he losing his mind? He could see Adonis looking at him, smirking and telling him that these men didn't care about him. "You're lying. He's standing behind you."

"Giovanni, there's no one in the room other than you, me, Dante, Niccolo, Romeo, Cutter and Blade," GianMarco pointed out.

Giovanni didn't appreciate the younger vampire's patronizing tone. He wanted to rip, kill, and maim, but he couldn't move. The hold these blasted warlocks had on him was too strong. He strained against its force and finally managed to move his head, otherwise he remained frozen to the spot. He saw everyone through a red filter as his rage boiled over. "You won't trick me. I see him. He's standing right there. He's right behind Romeo." He would have pointed but he wasn't able to.

Adonis chuckled. "They're lying, Giovanni. They know I'm here. They're just fucking with your mind. They don't want to see you get better. They want to hurt you. Don't believe anything they tell you."

Romeo scrunched his face in disbelief. He turned and waved at the air. His hands sliced right through Adonis whose image wavered slightly.

Giovanni blinked hard and Adonis disappeared. "Where? Where did he go? You destroyed him!"

Dante shook his head. "No. He was never there. He's dead, Giovanni. And he's never coming back."

"No!" Giovanni cried in agony.

Dante nodded. "Yes. He's gone."

"I...I killed him," Giovanni said the words out loud for the first time. They pained him more than any physical damage he'd inflicted on himself.

"He had to be stopped, Giovanni. Adonis has no one to blame but himself. It's not your fault. You did all that you could for him. Sometimes there are people who can't be saved. You we're a loving brother to him and I believe he knew that. No matter what he'd become, there was something within him that still loved you. Before he died, he wanted you to be the one to take him out because he felt your love for him. He knew you would do it with compassion and you gave him that beautiful gift. He died with a smile on his face because he was happy that you were there. He's in a better place now. Away from the darkness."

Tears cascaded down his face. "He can't be gone. Please tell me this is all a nightmare and I'll wake up any second."

Dante placed his hands on Giovanni's shoulders. "He's gone and never coming back. Remember him as he was and not what he'd become. Would the man he used to be want you to carry this much pain? You did the best you could, and you can't keep blaming yourself for the choices he made."

Niccolo, GianMarco and Romeo surrounded him "He was my best friend. You'll never know him as I did."

Romeo rubbed his back. "It's okay that you loved him. But I'm sure he loved you too and wouldn't want you to suffer like this."

"I have no one now," Giovanni whispered in defeat.

Dante shook his head vehemently. "That's not true. You have Sydney. She's your bloodmate. And you have us. We're your brothers and we love you Giovanni. You'll never be alone again."

Suddenly a wave of pure agony hit him, but it wasn't a physical pain, it was a spiritual. "Oh, God. My big brother is deeeeaaaaaadddddd!" He cried out.

The warlocks must have released him from their hold because Giovanni found himself collapsing but he didn't crash to the ground. Instead he was pulled into strong arms. Giovanni barely registered that Dante held him up. He released the misery he'd felt from the second Adonis's heart had stopped beating. The guilt had literally been eating him alive. Though he cried for Adonis's physical death, he was finally able to acknowledge that the brother he knew died a very long time ago. That he couldn't do more still weighed heavy on his heart.

He cried until his eyes burned and his throat was raw. Slowly, as his sobs subsided, his claws and incisors retracted. By the time the last tear fell, he felt shattered and weak. Briefly he lifted his head and standing across the room was Adonis, not the evil, twisted version, but the young, carefree boy. His best friend. The boy smiled and waved before disappearing.

"Goodbye Adonis," Giovanni whispered before everything went black.

Dante wasn't sure if Giovanni was completely out of the woods as far as his illness went but he believed the worst part was over. "We should take him to the car and head back to the women. The sooner we can reunite him with Sydney I think the faster he can completely heal."

GianMarco sighed. "I still believe he'll carry this guilt around for a while."

Dante nodded. "Considering all that he's been through, that's understandable. Come on, let's get going."

Dante's phone began to vibrate. He forgot to leave it in the car when he'd come in. He quickly checked it to see that it was Isis. "Yes, Isis?"

"We have a problem," Isis said without preamble.

"What's the matter?"

"Sydney is gone. And we can't find her anywhere."

## Chapter Nineteen

"Where are we going? I feel like we should have been home by now." Sydney could barely keep her head up. It was throbbing so bad she wanted to vomit. She wasn't sure how she'd wound up in a car driving to God-knows-where. Yet here she was in Dylan's old pick-up truck wedged between him and Ida.

Dylan rubbed her thigh. "Don't you worry about it, babe, we're just going for a little ride to calm your nerves. You've been having little episodes lately."

Sydney rubbed her temples. That didn't sound right. "Episodes? What are you talking about? Shouldn't we go to a doctor?"

Ida took her hand. "I already told you, Sydney, you've already been to the doctor. He couldn't find what was wrong with you, so we're taking you to a place where you can get the best care possible."

"But where?" Sydney demanded.

Dylan dug his fingers into her thigh, squeezing until she gasped in pain. "Relax and enjoy the ride. You're asking way too many questions."

Sydney attempted to pull away from his grip but he held her firmly. "Let go."

"Never," he declared.

"Dylan, you shouldn't be so rough with Sydney, especially in her fragile state." Ida spoke the words so indulgently one would think he was perpetrating some minor offense instead of outright assault.

Sydney felt uncomfortable and she wanted to go home. And one thought that remained constant in her mind was John. She didn't know why she kept thinking about him. He was just a man who had come through town looking for a room but the house was fully occupied. Based on that one meeting though, he'd certainly left an impression on her. But that didn't matter. She wanted this crazy car ride to end.

"I don't want to go anywhere but home," Sydney asserted.

"Shut up, Sydney," Dylan growled.

"Stop the goddamn, car! Let me out!" Sydney screamed.

Before she knew what was happening, a balled fist slammed into the side of her face. "I told you to shut the fuck up! Now look at what you made me do. Shit. I'm trying to fucking concentrate on the road and you're pissing me off. Apologize!"

She clutched her face. What the hell was going on? What had happened to Dylan? As far as she knew he'd never been a violent person. Why did he attack her all of a sudden? Regardless of whether something was wrong with him, she refused to apologize. Dylan had laid hands on her. If she knew where her cane was, she'd grab it and beat the shit out of him with it. "Fuck you," she countered.

"Dylan!" Ida reprimanded. "Keep your hands to yourself. You will not touch her again, do you understand?"

"She's really pissing me off. I thought you said you fixed her."

"Shut up, Dylan," Ida yelled.

Sydney didn't know what they were talking about but from the sound of it she didn't think she would get any help from the woman who she thought was her friend.

In a desperate move to be free of these two, she reached for the steering wheel and yanked with all her might.

"What the fuck are you doing, you crazy bitch!" Dylan yelled.

The car swerved back and forth but Sydney clung to the wheel fearful that if she let go, there was no telling where they would take her.

Ida grabbed her arm. "Sydney, no."

Sydney was thoroughly fed up. She elbowed Ida in the chest but the sudden pain in her head made her scream. Despite this, she held on to the wheel and gave it one more powerful tug before the car began to spin.

"Shit!" Dylan screamed. The car slammed into something hard and then the horn started to blare and wouldn't stop.

Ida let out an eerie scream. "Dylan! Dylan! You killed him! You killed him."

Before she could figure out what was happening, Ida began to rain blows over Sydney's head. For an old woman she was surprisingly strong.

Sydney fought back as best she could but this time when the sharp pain returned it rendered her unconscious.

<><><><><>

The house was empty.

"Shit," Giovanni cursed in frustration. He was bone-weary and emotionally drained, but when he'd learned that Sydney had disappeared there was no way he was going to leave the search to his brothers. He automatically suspected Dylan. He wouldn't have put it past that creep to kidnap Sydney.

The entire Grimaldi clan along with the Romanov twins had decided to aid in the search. Giovanni thought they should check Sydney's house for any clues but there was no sign of life anywhere.

While the others were combing through the rest of the house, Giovanni checked the bedroom. When he came to Sydney's room, everything in it reminded him of her. He didn't know how he would survive if something bad happened to her. He should have gotten someone to watch over her in his place, but once he was in the midst of his illness, it was hard for him to think logically.

He ran his hand along the fluffy pink robe hanging on a hook behind the bedroom door. It was the same one she'd worn on the night they'd made love—a night she couldn't remember. There was something going on in this house and he was determined to find out what it was. It was possibly the only clue he had to saving Sydney.

"We've found something!" Cutter yelled from down the hall.

Giovanni rushed out of the room to locate the warlock. Everyone else in their search party had gathered at the end of the hallway in a room Giovanni knew was Ida's. He pushed his way through the crowd to see what Cutter had found.

"What is it?"

"This room is rife with black magic. Someone here has practiced it for a very long time. And look what we found beneath the floorboard." Blade pointed to a spot on the floor where one of the boards had been removed. Giovanni knelt down to see a box covered in a pentagram. His hands shook because he had a strong premonition about what was in this box. He'd given up black magic to keep himself from turning into the monster his brother had become, but its call was powerful. He took a deep breath and flipped the box open. He gasped. Inside were bones, a human finger, a vile of blood, and symbols of ones who used the dark arts. Giovanni's heart skipped a beat when he saw a picture of Sydney with a drop of blood in the center of the picture.

It suddenly occurred to him now why Sydney was getting headaches. She was being controlled. When he'd used the dark arts, he'd learned of a spell to manipulate another person to his will. All it required was the image of the person and a part of their essence. Whenever the person being controlled would try to assert their own will the spell would stop them by causing great pain.

It finally made sense why Ida was so hostile toward him. If she was practicing black magic than she would have recognized that he wasn't quite human even though he'd recently gone through that purge and had no abilities. It was possible she believed that he would catch on to her little game. So while this woman had been working under the guise as Sydney's friend and right-hand woman, she was literally controlling her.

"That old bitch," He roared

"Can someone explain what all this stuff means?" Christine was the first one to speak.

"We'll have to explain that later. For now, we have to get to Sydney."

"I agree," a new voice to the group said.

Everyone turned around to see Nya enter the room.

When Sydney gained consciousness she felt the sensation of being dragged on the ground. Someone had her by the collar, making it hard for her to breathe. She gasped for air as she fought against the hold on her. "Be still. What I need to do won't take long at all."

It was Ida!

Everything came to her. Dylan and Ida had kidnapped her and there had been a car accident. Angered by what this woman had let her grandson do to her, Sydney planted her nails into Ida's hands and did her best to tear into her leathery flesh.

"You fucking bitch! I tried to be nice, but now you're pissing me off!" Ida released Sydney and smacked her across the face.

Sydney rolled away from her attacker and attempted to crawl away but Ida grabbed her by the ankle and yanked her along the hard earth floor. As far as Sydney knew, Ida was a frail old woman. How the hell was she this strong?

Sydney tried to grab anything she could get her hands on to make it hard for Ida to take her wherever she was trying to go. She wiggled, kicked and squirmed but the more she fought the tighter Ida's grip became.

"Stop fighting, bitch!" Ida screamed.

"Why are you doing this?"

"You killed my Dylan. All he wanted to do was love your blind ass but you couldn't accept that, could you? You thought you were too good for him. So what if he has a temper, who doesn't? You provoked him!"

"He fucking hit me and you let him! I thought you were my friend. You said I was like a daughter to you."

"That's right, you're exactly like my daughter Maureen. She was a defiant bitch too. The only good thing she ever did in her life was give me my sweet

Dylan and you killed him but I plan on fixing that," Ida explained as she continued to drag Sydney to wherever they were going.

"Here we are. Get up, bitch."

Sydney struggled to her feet. She turned to run but ran into what felt like a brick wall. She turned around and was met with another obstruction.

Ida laughed. "You're not going anywhere. You're trapped in my cube until I get back. Scream if you'd like. No one will hear you."

The sound of Ida's retreating footsteps told Sydney she was well and truly alone. "Help," she whispered.

<><><><><>

"Sydney is close, I can feel it," Giovanni said to no one in particular even though the car was full. There was a caravan of cars following the one he was in. Driven by Dante, he sat in the front passenger seat. The twins were in back.

"Are you sure?"

"I'm positive. She's in some sort of danger." Since the incident in the warehouse, Giovanni's connection to Sydney had grown stronger. Because he could think more clearly he was in tune with her.

The fact that they'd already made love meant that a bond had been established. He vaguely heard the word, help flicker into his mind. "I can hear her distress."

"Then we are indeed getting close," Cutter said. "As we continue in this direction, we're feeling some very powerful black magic. It's not as strong as the stuff we faced in Italy but this person is skilled in the arts. We'll have to tread carefully."

"You two along with Sasha should be able to counter anything Ida has in store for us."

Blade shrugged. "Maybe so but you know as well as us that there are parameters and rules in which our magic is used. There are no such requirements with the dark arts."

"Well I'll do whatever it takes to get her back. If that old bat harms one hair on Sydney's head she's fucking dead."

Anxiety struck him as the drive seemed to get longer.

*Help.*

There it was again.

Giovanni concentrated and attempted to reach out to his bloodmate. *Sydney, can you hear me?*

He got nothing but he refused to give up.

*Sydney if you can hear this, know that I'm on my way. I'll find you.*

There was still no answer. He grunted in frustration when he heard a very faint, *John?*

*Sydney is that you?*

*Yes. Am I going crazy? I hear you in my head.*

*That's because we're connected. Do you have any idea where you are?*

*How are you doing this? Yep. I'm definitely going crazy.*

Giovanni sighed. He'd been filled in on Sydney's time at the hotel. He was certain the women had explained the supernatural world to her, but apparently her memory had been wiped again. *Sydney, it's really me. We're on our way to get you. Just take a deep breath and tell me anything you can about your surroundings.*

There was a long pause and for a brief moment, Giovanni wondered if something had happened to her. *Sydney, are you there?*

*Yes. I'm here. I'm trying to listen for any clues. I'm outside because the wind is blowing all around me. But it feels like I'm trapped in a box of some sort. I hear birds and leaves rustling. I may be in a forest but I'm not certain. The truck crashed and the next thing I remember Ida is dragging me on the ground. She was so strong I couldn't fight her off.*

*And what about Dylan, is he lurking in the vicinity?*

*Ida said that Dylan is dead and that I killed him. I don't know where she's gotten off to but I think when she gets back she's going to....*

Panic rose in his chest.

*Sydney?*

There was no response.

*Sydney!*

Still not answer.

"Shit!" he said out loud.

"Did you connect with her?" Dante asked.

Giovanni racked his fingers through his hair in frustration. "Yes. She doesn't know where she is but she thinks she's outside. Ida must have her trapped by a spell. Sydney also mentioned an accident. She says that Dylan is dead and Ida is blaming her. I think Ida may try to hurt her."

"Well it's helpful that we know there's been an accident," Blade pointed out. "That way, we have a good chance of locating the abandoned vehicle. If you could tell us what Dylan's vehicle looks like we can try to pinpoint its location."

Giovanni desperately searched his memory for a description of Dylan's truck. "There's a detached garage in the back of Sydney's house and that's where people with vehicles parked. I do remember seeing a black pickup truck. It was an older model but I wouldn't be able to tell you the make or model."

"Dante, turn on the radio. I can enchant it to pick up the police airwaves within a hundred mile radius. Surely there will be news of an accident if there was a fatality," Cutter added.

"Good idea." Once Dante turned the radio on, Cutter began to chant under his breath.

Dante patted Giovanni on the shoulder. "Don't worry. We'll find her."

"I hope so," Giovanni whispered, knowing that if Sydney didn't survive her ordeal he had no reason left to live.

## Chapter Twenty

Sydney pounded against the barrier holding her prisoner. It didn't feel solid like a wall, in fact it felt stretchy. Every time she hit it, the material would wobble a little more than the last time. The boundary seemed to be weakening. Realizing this, she struck out with more force until finally she fell forward. She could feel dirt and grass beneath her hands. Sydney couldn't see where she was going and didn't know where she was but she had to get moving before Ida returned.

Wobbling to her feet she placed her hands out to keep herself from bumping into something as she made her getaway. She was still trying to reconcile the voice in her head. Somehow she'd been able to communicate with John telepathically. Maybe she was going crazy. She'd heard that in extreme cases of distress people tended to hallucinate. That's the only explanation she'd had for having an entire conversation with someone who was nowhere near here. Even by some strange chance that the discussion she'd had in her head was real, no one was around to help her now. The only person she had to depend on was herself.

Sydney moved cautiously while trying to maintain a steady pace. A few times, she encountered something solid and rough, trees. There were lots of them. She paused when she heard a familiar sound. Sydney strained to make out what it was.

Cars!

She had to be close to a road. Figuring if she could make it there, she could flag down a vehicle and get help. Just as she started walking again, something hard slammed into her back. "Going somewhere? Did you think you could get away from me?" Ida demanded.

Sydney fell to the ground from the impact. However, she refused to go down without a fight. She kicked and flailed. Her foot connected with something solid which she assumed was Ida.

"Umph!" Ida cried. "You'll pay for that."

Sydney tried to crawl away from but Ida hooked her arm around Sydney's neck. "Get off me," she yelled and clawed at her adversary's hands. But the harder she struggled the tighter the grip around her neck became. It became more difficult to breath and she was quickly losing strength. As she struggled for air, Sydney found herself drifting off into the abyss.

"There it is!" On the side of the road was three police cars and an ambulance surrounding a black truck. From the looks of things, the vehicle had smashed into the road's divider on the driver's side. The impact must have been hard because half of the car was completely caved in. Sydney had mentioned that Dylan was dead and witnessing this wreckage, Giovanni could see why.

The road thankfully didn't have a lot of traffic, which enabled them to pull over. The other cars in their caravan followed suit. "Dante, I need you and the others to clear out the police officers and the rest of the emergency workers. I'm going to see if I can locate Sydney on foot. Her presence is strong in this area."

"Okay. As soon as we clear everyone out, we'll join you."

Giovanni couldn't get out of the car fast enough. Nya appeared beside him. She'd been in her own vehicle. "I'm coming with you."

He nodded in acknowledgement. Giovanni couldn't tell if his friend was angry with him for letting Sydney get into a situation like this because she didn't say one way or another. But he had a feeling they'd have a long talk when this was all over.

As they moved forward they ran into a foul-smelling mist. "It's sulfur," he whispered. Usually that scent was strong when there was a demonic presence around.

"Shit!" Nya exclaimed. "We have to hurry!"

<><><><><>

Sydney gagged as smoke surrounded her. She was torn between gasping for air and holding her breath because the scent was noxious. She wanted to throw up. Ida had tied her up against a tree so she couldn't move her arms. It was so restricting the cords cut off her circulation. "Ida, let me go! What you're doing is wrong."

"Shut up! You were wrong for killing my Dylan. All you had to do was keep your mouth shut but you just had to provoke him. I've always looked out for you Sydney, I wouldn't have allowed him to hurt you."

"But you did! He hit me and you just sat there and did nothing. What kind of woman are you to allow that to happen? Why would you want me to be with an abusive person like Dylan?"

"Shut your goddamn mouth. My Dylan was just stressed. Do you know what it's been like for him? He was such a sweet little boy but my daughter was no damn good. I should have aborted her ass when I had the chance."

Sydney winced. "That's how you talk about your own daughter?"

Ida snorted. "I tried to love her but she was defiant and strong-willed since the day she was born. She hated reservation life. Thought she was too good for it. Always taking off with no-account men who only wanted to get in her pants. She was the reason my husband left, because she was nothing but trouble."

Sydney gasped and immediately coughed as she inhaled the disgusting smoke. Ida rarely talked about the daughter she'd lost, but Sydney couldn't remember her ever saying such horrible things about her own flesh and blood. This Ida was not the kind old woman who'd befriended her shortly after she'd gone blind. This wasn't the woman who had been her best friend for the last several years. This woman was a monster.

"So you dote on Dylan because you failed your own daughter?"

Sydney didn't hear Ida move before she felt the sharp sting of Ida's backhand.

"Watch your mouth! I didn't fail my daughter. Maureen was a whore who met the bad end that she'd been asking for all her life. And even though she didn't deserve it, Dylan actually loved that bitch. My sweet Dylan, who only wanted love. Maureen didn't give a shit about him. The Elders in our tribe wanted to lock Dylan away for a few minor transgressions. They forced us to move off the reservation. Even Dylan's own good-for-nothing father wouldn't acknowledge him. He lived a comfortable life with his family and treated my Dylan horribly. Those deaths weren't Dylan's fault. He didn't know anyone was in that house when he set fire to it. He was just trying to get back at his father for hurting him," Ida screamed the words. At this point Sydney didn't think the older woman was talking to her. These were the ramblings of a mad woman.

A chill ran down Sydney's spine. Dylan killed someone? How had he avoided jail? "He murdered someone?"

"He didn't mean to! They should have smelled the smoke and got out of the house when they had a chance. That man shouldn't have turned his back on my poor sweet Dylan. Just like that bitch of an ex of his shouldn't have tried to press charges against him. She had too much mouth if you ask me. She wouldn't stop talking. He didn't mean to strangle her!"

What the hell was Ida talking about? "If he killed all those people then how was he still free?"

"Because I have ways of manipulating situations." Ida sounded quite proud of herself.

"I don't believe you." Sydney gasped for air, feeling dizzy from all the smoke.

"Why not? I've been doing it to you for years. I knew a woman who showed me how to perform the dark arts. I knew I'd do whatever it took to protect my sweet Dylan and give him all the love he didn't get from my cunt of a daughter and his loser father. I would give him the world if I needed to. And for some reason he wanted your pathetic ass. He saw you before I introduced myself to you, you know. Said it was love at first sight."

"So you only became my friend so he could get close to me?"

"Why else would I attach myself to a blind little nobody? Now shut up. I have work to do."

This woman was clearly insane. The Ida she thought she knew didn't exist. And if what she said was true, she'd been covering for a murderer for years. It turned Sydney's stomach that she'd let Ida and Dylan get so close to her. Why didn't she see through their deception? Tears rolled down her face. The last several years of her life had been one big lie.

"So you're going to kill me, now?"

"Yes, but the bright side, your death will be for the greater good. I need to make a sacrifice in order to bring my Dylan back so that the spirits can be appeased."

Sydney struggled against her restraints but they seemed to tighten the more she fought.

Ida let out a loud evil cackle. "Fight all you like but you won't escape. Prepare to meet your end, bitch!"

"The only one who's going to meet her end is you!" A newcomer joined them.

John!

The smoke was thicker and the smell was almost unbearable as Giovanni and Nya got closer to the sound of a screaming woman. It was Ida, declaring her plans for Sydney. The second he heard the word sacrifice, he sped up not stopping until he spotted Ida's shadowy figure.

His heart nearly stopped beating when he saw the sight before him. Ida stood over Sydney who was bound to a tree. Ida held a large black dagger and it was clear she had every intention of using it.

Without hesitation, he made his presence known.

"John!" Sydney screamed his name.

Ida turned her head just in time for Nya to flash forward and knock her down with a powerful blow to the face. The old woman crumpled to the ground. "She's out cold," Nya stated, staring down at Ida's prone body with disgust. "But who is that?" She pointed to a body several feet away.

For the first time Giovanni saw Dylan's still form. His skin was ashen and his chest didn't rise or fall indicating he was not drawing breath. He was bloody and broken. It was a wonder how Ida had managed to get his body out of the vehicle before the police arrived but Giovanni figured she'd used some kind of black magic.

Having practiced black magic before, Giovanni immediately knew what Ida's intentions had been. She'd planned to sacrifice Sydney's life in order to resurrect Dylan. Thankful that Nya had knocked the old bitch out, he rushed to Sydney's side.

"What's going on?" Sydney's head went from side to side as if she were trying to listen out for what was happening.

"Sydney, I'm here." Giovanni frantically tore at her bonds and freed her. Then he pulled her into his arms and squeezed her tight.

"John? Is this really you?"

"Yes, Sydney. I'm here and I'm not going to let anything bad happen to you ever again."

She coughed before wrapping her arms around him and burying her face against his neck. "Thank you for saving me."

He stared down at her, happier than he'd felt in a long time. Just being in her presence was like a soothing balm to his aching heart. "No. You're the one who saved me."

"I hate to break up the reunion but we're going to need to get Sydney away from that thing." Nya nodded in the direction of Ida's still prone body.

Her body emitted a greenish light before it began to split in half. A large black slimy hand emerged from the now dead body.

It was a demon. Black magic was dangerous to anyone dared to use it but it was especially so for humans because it attracted demons. Once that demon attached itself to its host, the only way to extract it was by killing the host.

"We'll take care of this. We figured you might need our help." Blade appeared followed by Cutter and Sasha.

"John? What's happening?" Sydney asked in confusion.

"I have to get you out of here."

Giovanni looked over his shoulder in time to see the demon in its full form. The remains of Ida's body lay at its feet. The creature was nowhere near as big of the one that his mother had harbored so it would at least be easy to defeat. Sasha, Cutter, and Blade surrounded it and then sent a huge explosion of light from their fingertips bringing the monster to its knees.

"Let's go before the big explosion."

"Explosion?" Sydney asked

Just then the demon let out an unearthly sound that shook the ground.

"I'll explain later but for now. We have to go." Giovanni scooped Sydney up into his arms and started to run with Nya on his heels. He kept going until he spotted the caravan of vehicles on the side of the road. Dylan's pickup truck was in the same spot but all the emergency workers had left.

Dante spotted him first. "We were on our way to help you guys, but I see that you've found Sydney. What about the others?"

"Sasha and the twins are taking care of the demon. Thankfully it seems like a small one," Nya answered.

"I'm going to get Sydney home. Do you guys think you can handle the cleanup?"

"Sure."

"You can ride with me," Nya offered.

Giovanni looked down at the trembling Sydney, who clung to him for dear life. He placed a kiss on the top of her head. For the first time, he noticed the huge dark bruise forming on the side of her face. He didn't know if Ida or Dylan had been responsible for that mark but he wished he could kill them all over again. Sydney appeared to be in shock from the way her she shook in his arms.

Giovanni followed Nya to her vehicle, a large black SUV, and slid in the backseat with Sydney.

Just as they were about to pull away there was a loud blast coming from the area they'd left the demon. It seemed to shake Sydney out of her stupor. She let out a scream.

Giovanni clutched her hand. "Sydney! It's going to be all right. You're safe now. No one can harm you ever again."

"John?" she whispered with uncertainty in her voice.

He brought her hand to his lips and planted a gentle kiss on her knuckles. "Yes, I'm here, *amore*."

"Giovanni...?" She called him by his real name this time.

"Sydney."

She turned her head in his direction. "I remember," she said in wonder. "I remember everything."

## Chapter Twenty-One

Sydney stayed in the shower for as long as she dared. There were people waiting for her downstairs and she was in no particular hurry to get to them. Sure she wanted answers, but she still needed to wrap her mind around the events of today. Finding out that supernatural beings walked the Earth was only the tip of the iceberg.

As the spray of the shower cascaded over her head, the water masked the tears that fell. It broke her heart to learn that her dear friend had been using her all these years. All the times Ida had told Sydney she was like a daughter had been a lie. All those years when she'd laughed and cried with that woman, all Ida wanted was to play matchmaker between Sydney and her psycho grandson. She shuddered as she thought about the murderer she'd harbored in her house all this time. Now that she thought about it, she wondered if Dylan even had a job. Whenever he'd gone away had probably been an excuse to lay low from his crimes while Ida worked her black magic.

Now that her memory was back, it wasn't hard to imagine Dylan was capable of burning down a houseful of people. That he'd killed his last lover made Sydney shudder. There was no doubt that she would have been his next victim. She could clearly recall the incident of Dylan and the musician at the bar. She'd always wondered why her friend had never pressed charges. And now she realized Ida must have gotten to him somehow. She must have also figured out a way to manipulate the police.

The worst part of it all was that Dylan had laid hands on her before but Ida had wiped her memory of the incidents. He'd get angry with her for some minor offense, hit her, and promise to never do it again. But not one to take anyone's abuse, she'd break up with him, he'd go away for a while, Ida would erase her memory and the cycle would go on for years. Sydney was surprised that Ida hadn't cleared her memory of the incident at the bar. Maybe it was because Dylan hadn't actually touched her that time around.

She didn't like the idea that she'd been manipulated and lied to all these years, which made her think of John Chandler, also known as Giovanni Grimaldi. Even if he'd had the best of intentions, in a way he'd manipulated her too. He didn't trust her to at least tell her what was going on. While the whole vampire thing was still something she needed to come to terms with, she wasn't sure what she felt for him when a lot of what he'd told her were lies. The car ride to her house had been tense. Her memory had come back in a rush, making her dizzy.

*Sydney clutched her head. "I remember everything," she whispered with a frown. She remembered the hotel, Dylan's numerous offenses of violence against her and how Ida had basically looked the other way while her grandson was abusing her. But most of all she remembered every single moment she'd shared with Giovanni. As the woman who called herself Nya drove them back to her house, Sydney huddled in the back of the car as far away from Giovanni as she could. When he'd sat in the back with her and tried to hold her hand she'd snatched it away. She wasn't sure how she was supposed to feel because she wanted to know how much of what he'd told her was true and how much had been a cover for his alias John Chandler.*

"*Sydney, how are you feeling?*" *Giovanni touched her shoulder, but she flinched away.*

"*How do you think I'm supposed to feel? I've been lied to all these years by a woman I considered my best friend, who by the way tried to kill me because I stood up to her maniac grandson. Not to mention, this same woman has been erasing my memory for years. Now I don't know what's real and what's not. Oh, and do I even have to bring up the fact that I recently learned that there are vampires, witches and shifters?*"

*He released a heavy sigh.* "*I understand it's a lot to take in, but please know that everything I told you was true. I've lived a very long time Sydney and I've had many aliases over the years. For what I had to do, it was necessary. I'm sorry I had to lie to you about my name but that's it.*"

"*You also lied about your background story. Making money on the stock market indeed.*" *She snorted.*

"*Okay, that was also a falsehood but I promise you that's it.*"

"*Why? Why me? Why did you come to my house in the first place?*"

"*He did it as a favor to me,*" *the woman named Nya spoke up.*

"*And who are you?*" *Sydney demanded, more confused than ever.*

"*I'm Nya. I've been watching out for my family for a very long time. You're my last living descendent so naturally I'd have an interest in you.*"

*The woman's statement sent a chill up her spin, reminding her that these beings didn't live within the laws of nature.* "*How is that possible?*"

"*I wasn't always a vampire. I was human once. I had a child and he was taken from me. I eventually found him again but by then he had a family of his own and ultimately his children had children and so forth. But you're the last in my* line. I asked Giovanni to keep an eye on you because I felt that he was in a better frame of mind."

"Well, you were mistaken. Did you know what he did to those poor cops? Who's to say he won't go berserk again?"

"That will never happen again, Sydney. If you'll only let me explain it to you." Giovanni attempted to grab her hand again, but she yanked it away.

"Don't touch me. I don't know you."

"You do know me. I'm the same man who you kissed so sweetly and made love with until you cried out my name."

"Yeah, your alias." She returned her attention back to the woman. "Nya, what exactly were you going through that you couldn't check on me yourself?"

"The truth is, we've met before."

Sydney shook her head. "I think I'd remember that. You have a very distinct voice."

"I'm also good at disguising it," Nya said. "Do you remember an enthusiastic college student who sold magazine subscriptions?"

Sydney searched through the reserves of her memory and gasped. "That was you? Why didn't you say anything then?"

"Would you have believed me?"

"Probably not, but you still didn't answer my question."

"Oh? About why I didn't keep watch over you? It's because I'd recently lost someone. I wouldn't have been useful to you. I was so focused on how I was feeling that I selfishly didn't take Giovanni's feelings into consideration. You see the person I lost was my bloodmate, but that man was also Giovanni's brother."

Sydney licked her suddenly dry lips. "So it's true about you losing your brother?"

"Yes."

"And he meant that much to you?"

"Yes. It's one of the reasons the illness I suffered through was so intense. The guilt was killing me. I refused to accept *that he was gone and I simply couldn't let go. It's still hard to reconcile that he's dead and I was the one who killed him."*

*This was certainly a surprise turn of events. "Why? If you loved him so much why did you kill him?"*

*Giovanni sighed. "Adonis wasn't himself for a very long time. He did some very bad things. He killed innocents and would have continued doing so if I hadn't stopped him. Keep in mind, I'm almost eight hundred years old and though he was older than me chronologically, I was older than him in vampire years. I was the one who made him. There's always a bond when blood ties are involved, but the fact that I was his maker made it even stronger. When I killed him, a part of me died too and despite all the evil he'd perpetrated, I still loved him for the brother I once knew. Even when he committed one horrific crime after another, I never gave up hope that he could be good again. He used to be caring and very giving, but then he changed."*

*"Why did he change?" Sydney wanted to know.*

*"Our mother wasn't a good person. She used and manipulated his mind. She brainwashed him and persuaded him to perform unnatural acts with her."*

*"Unnatural acts? Do you mean him and her....?"*

*"My mother was a very sick woman."*

*"She was a vampire as well?"*

*"No, she was very much human."*

*Sydney scrunched her nose in confusion. "But you said she died recently. How is that possible if she wasn't...was she a witch or a shifter?"*

*"No, she practiced the dark arts. She learned a spell that would keep her youthful appearance for as long as she wanted it. But in order for this to happen, she took human sacrifices."*

*"That's awful."*

*"Yes. But the problem with the dark arts is there is always a price to pay. When a human practices this dangerous medium they attract demons who feed off that evil. In the end,*

she was done in by the monster who was lurking within her for centuries. It's not likely that your friend Ida was practicing as long as my mother, otherwise the demon that had attached itself to her would have been much bigger."

Sydney flared her nostrils in anger. "Don't call that bitch my friend."

"My apologies. I only wanted to give you a little background."

She still had so many questions. "Why do you know so much about black magic?"

"Because I used to practice it myself."

"And did you attract a demon?"

"No. I'm immortal. That only happens to humans who dabble in it. But there are still side effects. It can change one's personality, make them paranoid, crazed and dangerous. Adonis practiced it, and I took up the art to keep one step ahead of him. Shortly before I came to your house, I'd had a purge performed to cleanse me of the darkness. That's why I slept three days straight. I literally hadn't slept in years. That's what black magic can do to a person, which is why it shouldn't be messed with."

"Okay, I sort of understand your reasoning for everything else but why couldn't you have just watched me from afar?" What she didn't add was that by entering her life he'd turned it upside down. She didn't know him well but that pull she felt toward him couldn't be denied. Even still, with all that had happened recently, she seriously doubted they had a future together.

"We do have a future together, Sydney. You're my bloodmate. I tried to fight it from the moment I laid eyes on you because I didn't feel like I deserved a happily ever after but having nearly lost you, I don't intend to ever let you go again."

"Get out of my head. You don't have permission to read my mind. You speak as if I don't have a say in the matter. I've *gone through a life-altering experience and I need time to work through some things."*

*"We'll work through them together."*

*"You keep saying 'we' like there's an 'us.'"*

*This time when Giovanni caught her hand, he refused to let go. "You are the woman I've waited for nearly a millennium. You are my bloodmate, Sydney, and deny it all you want, but we belong together and we will be.*

Sydney felt somewhat better by the time she stepped out of her shower. The Grimaldi clan had all insisted they come by her house to make sure everything was all right. It wasn't as if she could tell them "no" after all they'd done for her. She didn't particularly feel like playing hostess right now but she could no longer keep them waiting.

When she stepped into the bedroom with a towel wrapped around her naked body she halted when she made it to the center of the room. She wasn't alone. But Sydney instantly knew who it was. She could smell his unique scent, and his presence was larger than life, he didn't need to say a word for her to know he was there.

Sydney clutched the towel around her body in a death grip. "Get out," she ordered.

"Not until we've talked."

"There's nothing to talk about, Giovanni. We've already discussed all that's needed to be said in the car."

"Maybe you have, but I have plenty to say, Sydney. I know —"

"I'm sure you have a lot of flowery words in your arsenal because after all you have lived a very long time. I bet you think this poor blind girl doesn't stand a chance, but I'm not going to allow anyone else to dictate my life again. So you can keep this bloodmate bullshit to yourself. Now leave my room please. I have guests waiting for me."

Giovanni was silent but she didn't hear him move an inch.

"Didn't you hear me?"

"I head every word you said." His voice sounded strained as if he was trying to hold himself in check.

"Then go."

"You don't have any guests to go downstairs to. I sent them back to the hotel. They'll be in town for a few more days so there will be plenty of time for you to speak with them."

Once again, she felt manipulated and her patience was already short. Sydney moved closer to the sound of his voice and when she felt his heat, she stopped in front of him and poked her finger into his chest. "You had no right."

"I had every right, Sydney. You're mine and we needed to be alone. They all understood."

"I'm yours? Now you sound like Dylan."

He grasped her shoulders. "Don't you dare compare me to that motherfucker. I would never lay a hand on you."

"How do I know that? We barely know each other."

"But our hearts are very well acquainted. Should I remind you of how good it was between us…how good it can be?"

"Don't you dare, I swear I'll scream," she threatened.

"That's what I'm aiming for Sydney. I want you to scream at the top of your lungs because I'm about to claim you heart, body and soul. I've spent the majority of my life fighting for other people, denying myself the simplest of pleasures, but not anymore. This time I'm going to fight for myself. For us. So the only words that will stop me from devouring every inch of this delectable body is that you don't want this."

Sydney opened her mouth to say exactly that, but no words came out. She tried again, but immediately pressed her lips together.

With a growl, Giovanni scooped her off her feet and carried Sydney across the room before dropping her on the bed.

## Chapter Twenty-Two

Giovanni didn't give Sydney a chance to change her mind because he immediately slid on top of her and covered her slightly parted lips in a hungry, desperate kiss. He'd missed the taste of her. She was sweeter than the rarest honey. Though he was over the worst part of his illness, it wasn't completely out of his system, but by the time he finished thoroughly claiming her it would be.

This time he wasn't worried about having an accident like he had before because the beginning stages of *la morte dolci* was the worst. At least now he had full control of his faculties...except for his cock which was rock hard. He wanted to slip into her tight pussy right now but not before he had a chance to sample every part of her with his hands and mouth.

He outlined the seam of her lips with his tongue, reveling in their fullness before slipping inside the warm cavern of her mouth. He swallowed her breath, wanting to consume her, be one with her.

Sydney moaned, threading her fingers through his hair. She pressed her tongue forward to meet his, tentatively at first but she then she grew bold, swirling it around his. Their tongues danced, circling, licking and tasting. An immeasurable wave of pleasure swam through his body. Her mouth wasn't enough. Giovanni wanted more. Needed it. Craved it. He broke off their kiss, gasping for air as he cupped her face between his palms. He stared into her beautiful brown eyes. Everything about this woman was pure perfection.

"You're so fucking beautiful. And you're mine." He planted kisses all over her cheeks, necks and nose. He loved the feel of her soft skin beneath his lips. Giovanni ran his tongue along the vein in her neck, feeling her pulse. It sped up under his caress.

"Giovanni, what are you doing to me?" she groaned.

"Making you feel good, I hope."

"You are, but—"

"No buts. Just feel."

He pulled back just enough to rip the towel from her body. He wanted to see every inch of her. Once she was completely naked beneath his gaze, Giovanni feasted on the sight of her. He admired her full round breasts and slightly rounded belly. Just below that was a soft patch of hair, guarding her most precious gift.

Sydney trembled as if she were afraid.

"*Amore*, why are you shaking?"

"Because I'm scared."

"Of what?"

"Of what you think of me, of my body."

He cupped one firm breast in his palm, making Sydney gasp. He brushed his thumb against her nipple, watching it pucker beneath his tongue. "I think you're beautiful, Sydney. I've made no secret of how perfect I think you are. I love this freckle on your right breast." He then leaned down to kiss it.

"I love this scar on your shoulder." Giovanni ran his tongue over the wound which looked old, probably from a childhood accident. "I love these nipples. The color of coffee but so much sweeter." He dipped his head and sucked each one in turn.

Sydney tugged at his hair so hard that he thought she'd rip some of it out of his scalp but he didn't mind. He loved how responsive she was to his tongue. The last time they were together so intimately, he'd made her come with a little breast play. He wondered if he could do it again but this time with a bit more intensity.

Giovanni tugged one turgid tip between his lips and applied pressure. And he then began to suck more aggressively, nearly getting her entire breast in her mouth. While he did this, he plucked her other nipple between his fingers.

"Giovanni, I don't think I can take it," Sydney moved, rolling her head from side to side.

He lifted his head just enough to speak. "You're going to take it. All of it. I won't be denied this tour of your body." Giovanni continued to knead and nibble on her breast.

"All mine," he whispered.

"You sound so sure of that," she softly taunted.

"Goddamn right I am," he growled. "All of you belongs to me." He moved his hand lower to cup her sex. "This proves it. You're so wet, your juices are dripping down your thighs. Do you feel that, *amore*? Your heat is practically burning my hand."

Sydney squirmed and moaned. "I can't think straight when you do that. What are you doing to me?" she moaned.

"Making you feel good." His impatience was his undoing. Instead of remaining at her breasts, Giovanni made a descent down her body eager to taste more of her. He pressed a kiss in the valley of her breast before moving lower. He circled her belly button with his tongue. "You taste so good. Like the rarest of confections."

"Giovanni," she whispered his named, running her hands along his arms and back.

He pushed her legs apart and buried his nose against her pussy.

To his surprise, she scooted away. "No," Sydney whispered.

"No? You don't like this? Your body tells me otherwise."

"I do like it…it's just."

Giovanni stroked her soft cheek. "Tell me what you want, *amore*."

"You. I want to feel you too, touch you all over."

The idea of Sydney exploring his body was too much of a temptation to resist. "Then touch me, *amore*."

"No. Not like this."

"Then how?"

"I want to be on top."

A smile curved his lips as he pictured exactly that. "Okay, Sydney. I tell you what. You can get on top but you have to straddle my face."

Giovanni's grin widened when he spotted the blood rush to her cheeks.

"Giovanni, I…I've never done that before. I mean, what if I smother you?"

"Amore, I don't care, as long as it involves your pussy on my lips."

She hesitated for a moment, her uncertainty giving her an innocence that made Giovanni's already hard cock ready to burst.

"Okay," she finally answered. "What do I do?"

"Just sit back while I take off my clothes."

"No. Let me."

He gulped. "Okay." Giovanni slid off the bed and pulled Sydney with him. It took every ounce of his willpower not to toss her back on her on the bed and ravage this woman until her every waking thought was him.

With trembling fingers, Sydney moved her hand against his chest. Just a simple touch from her sent him close to the edge. She caressed his torso, exploring the plains of his body. Then she grabbed the hem and yanked it up.

She giggled. "You're going to have to help me with this."

Giovanni smiled. "My pleasure." He shrugged out of his shirt as she lifted it.

Sydney immediately went for his pants and quickly pulled them down. Once he kicked them off she touched the top of his thigh. She gasped. "You're not wearing any underwear."

"They're a nuisance." He barely got the words out as she circled his cock with her fingers.

To his surprise, Sydney went to her knees. In one hand she held his shaft and with the other she lightly stroked his length, almost with reverence. "It's so long and thick." Running her fingertip over the head, she touched him as if committing the shape of his dick to memory. "It's beautiful," she whispered. "You're already dripping." She caught a drop of his pre-cum with her fingertip.

She wrapped her lips around his member and slowly sucked into mouth, inch by excruciating inch.

"Sydney!" he cried out in surprise, delight and lust.

Sydney took him deep into her mouth before releasing him just until the tip remained and then she sucked him deep again. Slowly she worked his dick, her head bobbing back and forth in a slow steady pace. Giovanni held her head, guiding it back and forth. He was careful not to thrust forward so he wouldn't choke her but with each passing second it became impossible to remain still. She sucked and slurped as if she couldn't get enough.

When he saw Sydney gently squeezed his balls, Giovanni lost it. With a growl, he hauled Sydney to her feet before pushed her onto the bed. "On your hands and knees now."

"But I didn't get a chance to—"

"Now!" he roared.

"But Giovanni I—"

"If your pussy is not on my lips in five seconds, I'm going to paddle that ass so hard you won't be sitting for a week."

Sydney scrambled to get into position.

"Now spread your legs a little so I can see that pretty little pussy of mine."

Once again, she obeyed his command. Giovanni licked his lips in anticipation. The erotic sight of his dark-skinned beauty, eager and ready for him, was more than he could take. Giovanni slid onto the bed and positioned himself beneath her. He had a gorgeous view of her wet, puffy pussy lips, and a tight little rosette. Grabbing a handful of her ass he pulled her down until her pussy covered his mouth. He dove in and began licking and sucking. Her juices contained the life-giving essence that gave vampires their strength and vitality. He could eat this succulent treat for hours.

"Oh God!" She screamed. "Giovanni!" Sydney wiggled her hips, grinding against his face and slathering it with her wetness.

As he devoured her, he rubbed the tight ring of her anus with his thumb. He then rubbed it against her pussy, dampening it just enough to make it slick before returning it to her puckered bud. Slowly, he eased his thumb past the tight muscles.

She stiffened. "What are you doing?"

"Claiming every inch of you."

A shiver shimmed down her spine, making Sydney shake from desire. She'd never allowed anyone to play with her ass before but the wave of pleasure that coursed through her being would not be denied. She could barely concentrate with him doing suck decadent things to her body.

Wanting to finish what she'd started, Sydney returned to his cock and tested its weight in her palm. It was so large. She could only image what it looked like but she knew it was a thing of perfection. She loved its shape, from the velvety cap to the slightly curved shaft. She pumped it in her fist, loving the feel of the hard steel. Everything about this man turned her on. He engaged all of her senses, from the sound of his moans as he made a meal of her to the very masculine scent of him. Giovanni made her feel things she never thought herself capable of. And when she was with, he made her see colors like a prism.

She took him into her mouth again, reveling in the tangy, musky taste of him. He tasted amazing and she loved the scent of him as well. Sydney attempted to get as much of him in her mouth as she could. She noticed the more fervently she sucked him, the more frantic he became as he ate her pussy.

Sydney had never performed the 69 position with anyone before but now she wondered what else she'd been missing out on. The act of giving while receiving was a mind-blowing experience.

Just then Giovanni pressed his finger all the way into her bottom, making her cry out in surprise. And during this time, he continued to fuck her pussy with his tongue. It took Sydney a moment to adjust to this new sensation but when she did, it was like an awakening.

There were nerve endings inside of her that she hadn't been aware of, ones that curled her toes and made her purr. Slowly he moved that finger in and out of her rear as he captured her clit between his teeth. He nibbled on it gently at first before applying pressure. When he bit down, she released his cock and cried out. The pleasure-pain was just enough to shove her over the edge.

Sydney's climax rocked her to the core. With her arms too weak to support her weight, she fell forward, but Giovanni wasn't done. "Mine," he growled.

She pressed her head into the bed, still coming down from an amazing high.

Giovanni removed his finger and licked her from clit to anus. "So good."

"Can't. Take. It. Too. Much." Sydney moaned weakly, fighting for breath. The man would be the death of her. Were all vampires this insatiable?

Giovanni responded by smacking her on the rear. The sharp sting sent a pulse of pleasure to her clit. He popped her again. And again. Her ass was on fire, but it was the kind of hurt that felt good. So fucking good.

Another climax came quick and hard, making it difficult for her to even move.

He gently pushed Sydney off of him and rolled her onto her back. "Now I'm going make you mine completely and thoroughly. He hovered over her, the heat of his breath fanning her face. Giovanni nudged her thighs apart with his knee before situating himself between her legs.

She was already tender from his attentive mouth so when he placed the thick head of his cock against her entrance, Sydney cried out as she anticipated being so thoroughly filled by him.

Giovanni framed her face in his palms, "Are you ready for me, *amore*?"

"Yes, please. Give it to me."

He pushed into her with one powerful thrust.

"Giovanni! Yes!" He was so deep inside of her it almost felt like they shared a body.

"Mine, sweet Sydney," he groaned as he slowly started to move, sliding in and out of her sheath.

Each time he'd nearly pull out of her pussy and then slam back into her, making her feel pleasure in every cell in her body. She ran her fingers down his sweat-slickened back. Sydney lifted her hips to meet him thrust for thrust.

"Mine," he whispered in her ear.

Without warning Sydney felt a prick just above her collarbone. It took her a moment to realize what had happened. He bit her!

She stiffened, frightened that he might lose control, but slowly she relaxed as the pleasure intensified. As their bodies preformed an intimate dance as old as time, Sydney experienced wave after wave of unbelievable passion. She realized she could become addicted to this man and it frightened her. As that thought crossed her mind, a powerful orgasm swept through her with the power of a tsunami.

"Giovanni!"

He raised his head and screamed her name. "Sydney!"

Slowly she floated to earth with a smile on her lips. "That was...amazing."

Giovanni pulled her within the circle of his arms and she placed her head against his chest. Sydney had never felt safer than she did in this moment and it frightened the hell out of her. She wasn't supposed to have feelings for this man when their entire acquaintance had been based on a lie. Her heart told her one thing, but her head told her another. She was still trying to reconcile what Ida had done to her. How could she put her trust in anyone else?

"And that's how it will be for us for the rest of our lives."

She stiffened. "Giovanni...don't ruin the moment. Just because we had sex—"

"Don't you dare say it, Sydney. We belong together. It doesn't matter how long we've known each other, our hearts know the truth."

Tears stung her eyes. "Everyone I've ever loved is gone. And Ida....well, you see what happened with that situation. How do I know this won't eventually end? You're a vampire and I'm human. You'll live forever and I'll get old."

"You won't because I'll bring you over."

"What if I don't want to be a vampire?"

"We don't have to talk about it now, Sydney."

"But we will eventually. Look Giovanni, I have to get used to the idea of us. I haven't exactly had the best of luck with relationships and I'm not going to allow you to run my life. I may not have sight but I'm capable of handling myself."

Giovanni placed a gentle kiss on her lips. "Sydney, your independence is something I admire about you. I don't want to run your life, I just want to be a part of it. I want to be by your side for the rest of forever. Just say you'll give us a chance."

She'd never been more scared of anything in her life. But what terrified her the most was never feeling the way she felt with Giovanni ever again.

"Okay," she whispered. "But I just need some time."

## Chapter Twenty-Three

"Your family is really nice. I miss having them around," Sydney mused as she rocked back on forth on the new porch swing Giovanni had installed. Ida had been fond of the rocking chairs but Sydney had always wanted an old-fashioned porch swing. With Ida out of her house, getting rid of the rocking chairs on her front porch was one the first things she'd done to erase all traces of that evil old battle-ax.

"Me too." Giovanni joined her on the swing and draped his arm around her. "But remember, they're your family now as well."

Sydney liked the sound of that. She rested her head on Giovanni's shoulder, never wanting this feeling of pure and utter contentment to end. The Grimaldi clan had become a huge part of her life in the past couple of months. After what had happened with Ida and Dylan, they'd rallied around her in a big unit of support, giving Sydney the sense of family she'd missed since she'd lost her parents and sister.

Despite them being immortal beings, she couldn't have met a more genuine, loving bunch of people. They constantly called and checked in on her and visited often. Usually one or two of them would come at a time, but the last visit the entire family had converged on her. It had been like a huge family reunion. Sydney had grown particularly close to the women. Maggie, Sasha, Christine and Isis would never replace Tara, but they felt like sisters.

She adored the children. Gianna, Maggie and GianMarco's child was just learning to talk, and somehow 'shit' had become her favorite word, much to her parents' distress. Sydney was very much looking forward to Maggie's new baby who would be due in a few months. Christine and Romeo's children were precocious and adorable. Little Jaxson was something else, saying anything and everything that popped into his mind, while his little sister Adrienne was extremely loving and loved giving out hugs and kisses. Sydney finally had the pleasure of meeting Niccolo and Sasha's son Jagger along with his bloodmate Camryn. Jagger Grimaldi was just as charming as his uncles. Though Dante and Isis didn't have children yet, Isis had confessed that she was looking forward to having as many of her bloodmate's babies as she could.

It was clear for anyone around the Grimaldis that they were a family who loved and supported each other, and that they included Sydney with open arms was an honor. And even though she had been adopted into this family, she wouldn't have gotten over the ordeal of what Ida had done to her if it weren't for Giovanni. He had quickly become her rock.

In the beginning she was cautious, scared that he'd try to manipulate her or change who she was. But he neither smothered her nor ordered her around...unless they were in bed. She enjoyed that part. A lot.

When she'd wake up from a nightmare he was there to hold her close. Whenever she had a gig at the bar, he was there, listening and offering her support. Because of his encouragement she'd recently started writing music again which she hadn't done since before her accident.

She'd learned that Giovanni possessed a vast fortune and had properties all over the world, but he decided to move into her house while they developed their relationship. He wanted her to be comfortable and she was grateful that he'd allowed her to set the pace between them. It worked out for Sydney because she currently had no boarders. With the summer over, Katrina and Mikhail had returned home, and Peter's son had convinced him to move in with his family. Once they were gone, Sydney had decided not to take in any more boarders, at least until she decided what to do with the house. It no longer gave her the same pleasure it once did. It had soured for her. She wasn't sure if it was because of Ida and Dylan or that she was just ready to start a new chapter in her life, but lately she'd been considering selling it.

Giovanni massaged her arm. "You seem to be deep in thought. What are you thinking?"

Sydney leaned over and offered her lips to him which he quickly took in a deep, long kiss. "Mmm, that was nice," she said slowly pulling away from him. "I'm surprised that you didn't just read my mind."

He chuckled. "Oh, so you're teasing me now? I know better than to do that again."

The last time he'd read Sydney's mind without her permission she held out from having sex with him. Of course her sex strike only lasted an hour but Giovanni had acted as if it was the longest hour of his life.

"That's right, buster. Anyway, I was just thinking about how happy I am. Honestly I can't remember feeling this way since my family was alive. They would have liked you."

"You think so?"

"I know so."

"I wish I could have met them."

A smile touched her lips. It still made her sad knowing she'd never see them again, but the memories were no longer painful. "You would have liked them too. My dad loved telling corny jokes. It aggravated my mother but she put up with it because she loved him."

"They sound like they were amazing people."

"They were."

"My brother was pretty amazing too. Before he died."

Sydney placed at kiss on his cheek. "Adonis?" Giovanni didn't talk about the brother he'd lost often but whenever he did, she could always hear a deep sadness in his voice. It was obvious that he still hadn't gotten over Adonis's death, but it was a positive sign that he was starting to talk about him more often.

"Yes. Like your father, Adonis was fond of a good joke. He liked to pull pranks. His favorite target was our tutor. He gave that poor man hell." Giovanni chuckled. "Even though I fully understand that Adonis made his own choices, I still wonder at what point I could have helped him. I sometimes think, I should have tried harder to convince him to come with me when our father offered us refuge. Maybe even then I was too late because my mother had warped his mind so badly, I barely recognized him."

"You don't talk about your mother that often."

"That's because there's really not much to say about her. She was a very beautiful woman on the outside but on the inside, she was an ugly dark soul. Beatrice was a miserable human being because she was never satisfied."

"I notice you don't refer to her as mother."

"Because she was never really a mother to me."

"So you hated her?"

Giovanni sighed. "I wouldn't say that exactly. I hated the things she did, but I didn't hate her. I felt pity for her actually."

Sydney raised a brow. "Pity? But why? If she was as evil as you say, why spare her your empathy?"

"I pity her because she never really learned to value the things she had. It led to her destruction."

Sydney could understand that. "Like your brother, maybe something happened to her when she was younger to make her the way she was."

"That's quite possible but I guess I'll never know. I'd like to think she wasn't born evil."

"Me too. Speaking of mysteries, I wonder if we'll see Nya again." The female vampire had disappeared shortly after Sydney's rescue with no other explanation. She never did get to ask Nya the many questions she wanted answers to. Sydney would have liked to talk to her more, hear her story, but it was clear Nya wasn't ready to share it.

"I hope so. Like I was, she's in a lot of pain and just hasn't figured out how to deal with it."

"Won't you go looking for her?"

"Trust me, *amore*, if she doesn't want to be found I'll have to respect that. Long before she was a vampire, she suffered a lot. She's very tortured. But hopefully one day she'll learn to forgive herself as I have learned to let go of guilt."

"I hate that she's out there all alone."

"Me too. But something tells me she won't be alone for long."

"What do you mean?"

"Let's just say she may be in for a double dose of trouble."

Sydney wasn't sure what he meant by that, but Giovanni didn't sound particularly concerned about it. She was certain if he knew his friend was in any kind of danger he'd act on it. Sydney hoped wherever Nya was, she was okay.

A comfortable silence fell between them as they continued to rock back and forth, enjoying a moderate fall day. Sydney realized there was no place she would rather be than here with this man for the rest of her days. "Giovanni?"

"Yes, *amore?*"

"I need to tell you something."

He stroked her cheek. "You can tell me anything, Sydney."

"I just wanted to say that I love you. I know I've been holding back for a while now but I was just too scared to express my feelings. I didn't trust my heart because all that I've gone through, but I know I want to be with you forever. I wake up in the morning and you're the first thing on my mind, when I go to sleep you're my last thought, and when I'm sleeping I dream of you. I don't know what the future holds for me, but I know that I want to spend it with you." She exhaled. "There, I've said it. I've wanted to tell you that for weeks."

Giovanni remained silent.

"Giovanni?"

His lack of response made her nervous. Had he changed his mind about her? The anxiety was just too much. "Tell me I didn't just make a fool of myself by telling you how I feel."

"No," he whispered, his voice thick with emotion. "It's not that. Feel." He took her hand and brought it to his face. His cheeks were damp.

"You're crying? Why?"

"Because you have no idea how long I've waited to hear those words. Sydney, I've been through hell and back and the only thing that kept me going was the hope that one day I could unite my family. But when Adonis died, that dream was shattered. I didn't think I could ever be happy again or that I deserved it. And then there you were, like a beautiful dream. I'd seen you from afar and part of me already suspected that you were the one my heart had been waiting for. Meeting you was my greatest joy and pain because at the time I was going through too much to be any good for you. I fought against the idea of us as some form of punishment. But you healed me. I want to thank you and tell you that you mean the world to me. I can't say that I love you because love is not a powerful enough word for how I feel about you. I *can* tell you that you're my world, my breath, my heartbeat and my soul. For the first time in my life, I'm looking to forever because I'll be spending it with you."

By the time he finished his speech, Sydney's own tears fell freely. "Oh Giovanni." She leaned over and their lips collided for a long, slow deep kiss. Their tongues danced and swirled around the other.

The next thing Sydney knew, Giovanni had scooped her up and carried her into the house. He didn't take her upstairs as she expected him to. He walked inside and made an immediate left. The hum of the dishwasher alerted her to the room he'd stopped in. "Why are we in the kitchen?" she asked.

"Because I couldn't wait." He plopped Sydney on kitchen table and pushed her legs apart.

She'd never been more thankful in her life to be wearing a dress. Giovanni yanked her panties off with one powerful tug while she frantically unbuckled his pants. He couldn't get inside of her fast enough and when his hardness slipped deep inside her wet channel, Sydney sighed with relief. No matter how many times they made love, every time they were together was like the first time.

"So good." Sydney wrapped her legs around his waist and clung tightly to Giovanni as he stroked her with his big addictive cock. Making love had become their favorite pastime together. They'd fucked in every single room in the house excluding Ida's old room, which Sydney refused to step foot in.

"I love you so much," she moaned against his neck.

"You are my heart, forever." Each word was punctuated with a thrust. He was so deep inside of her, she wasn't sure where he ended and she began. They were one. Heart, body and soul. She'd follow this man to the ends of the earth.

An intense fire spread throughout her, burning so hot she thought she'd burst in flames. Sensation flared within her, shooting from the depth of her being.

"I can't hold on much longer," he moaned.

She clenched her muscles around his cock which sent Giovanni over the edge. He yelled his release, spilling his seed inside of her. "Sydney!"

She clenched him tighter still, milking his cock, and not wanting this moment to end.

"Come for me," he whispered against her ear.

It was all she needed to reach her peak. Her body shook as bursts of flashing light exploded all around her.

Sydney wasn't sure how long they remained locked together but she wanted to remain like this for as long as possible.

Giovanni planted a hard kiss against her lips. "You really are mine now. Forever. And I'll never let you go."

She smiled. "Promise?"

# Epilogue

Sydney blinked from the bright light being shined into her pupils. "Everything seems to be in order, Ms. Lewis. You've made a remarkable recovery. Better than I could have expected." Dr. Green smiled at her. She could actually see his smile!

Shortly after she finally declared her feelings for Giovanni, she realized she could make out bright lights. She didn't think anything of it because she'd experienced that after her last surgery. But then things became blurry and if she looked close enough she could just manage to make them out. Sydney didn't mention it to Giovanni at first because she didn't want to get her hopes up. But he noticed. It was he who had suggested that she was getting her sight back.

Giovanni had explained that she was probably supposed to get it back all along but Ida's interference had hindered her. It made sense that Ida somehow made it so that the operations were unsuccessful. Without her eyesight, Ida probably believed Sydney was more vulnerable and would be dependent on her. Sydney did rely on Ida but only because the other woman had insinuated herself so firmly into Sydney's life that she really had no choice.

Sydney's sight came back gradually. At first she could make out large items, but soon her focus had become sharper until her vision was nearly perfect. It was how she'd found herself back in Dr. Green's office.

"I can hardly believe it, Doctor. On our last visit, I'd given up all hope yet here I am."

Dr. Green patted her on the shoulder. "Everything looks good now but I'd like to see you back in six months to do another check-up. In the mean time I'll recommend you to an optometrist so you can get fitted for glasses to correct your vision to 20/20. I personally would not recommend contact lenses until you receive the all clear at our next appointment."

"Sure," she agreed, knowing that by then she wouldn't need any kind of eyewear.

"Well, if you have no more questions for me today, Ms. Lewis, I'll be seeing you in six months. Take care of yourself." He held out his hand and she gave it a brief shake.

"Thank you, doctor."

Sydney practically skipped out of Dr. Green's office. Having been blind for the last ten years, everything was like brand new to her; colors seemed brighter and everything fascinated her. Several times she'd made complete strangers uncomfortable because she couldn't stop staring at them. One of the first things she did was purchase a television, and she and Giovanni spent an entire week binge-watching shows on a streaming service. She loved going for walks and just seeing the world around her.

And the best part of getting her vision back was being able to actually see her handsome man with functional eyes. She scanned the waiting room and spotted Giovanni. He stood up when he saw her coming his way. As she got closer her heart skipped a beat. She couldn't believe this beautiful man was actually hers. She knew he was handsome even before she could actually see him, but she never thought he was a walking God.

The man was sex on two legs. His face was the kind that inspired artists to paint.

The entire Grimaldi clan was ridiculously good-looking which made her wonder if all immortals were as gifted in the looks department. Giovanni had laughed when she'd asked that question and had told her it was just genetics.

He smiled at her to reveal perfect white teeth. "How did it go?"

"Everything looks great. He wants to see me in six months, but I think I may skip that appointment. Because you know…" Sydney had decided she would allow Giovanni to bring her over. If she was going to be with him forever they might as well get that out of the way. She was still a little apprehensive about becoming a vampire but with Giovanni's guidance everything would be all right.

He cupped her face in his palms. "Yes. I know but we don't have to do this thing right away. We have time."

"No. I want to do it. This is a step toward our forever."

His jade green eyes glistened with the suspicious sheen of tears. "Oh, *amore*." He lowered his head and covered her lips with his. Sydney wrapped her arms around his neck and pressed her body against his, eagerly returning his kiss.

"Hey, this is a doctor's office, not a hotel. Get a room," a lady in the waiting room yelled at them.

They pulled away from each other, giggling like two naughty children.

Giovanni smiled and held out his hand to her. "Let's go home and celebrate properly."

Sydney placed her hand in his. "I thought you'd never ask.

<><><><><>

"You'll love living around here. It's nice and quiet and so many shops! Can you imagine all the shopping trips we can go on together?" Maggie gushed.

GianMarco rolled his eyes. "Do you see what's happening? They're already trying to corrupt your poor bloodmate. Sydney doesn't stand a chance around those four." He pointed in the direction of the woman who were gathered on the other side of the room. Sydney sat in the middle, looking through a catalogue of potential plots to build their house on.

Giovanni looked on at his bloodmate with a smile on his face. He loved that woman so much it almost hurt. As if sensing his stare, she raised her head and smiled at him. She blew him a kiss before returning her attention back to Maggie, Sasha, Christine and Isis, who were plotting another shopping excursion at this very moment. His brothers had warned him that the women were black belt shoppers but he knew none of them would begrudge their women anything. And whatever made Sydney happy made Giovanni happy. Besides, everything he had was hers. He'd give her the world if she asked for it.

Sydney had decided she no longer wanted to live in her house anymore because of too many bad memories. Giovanni couldn't blame her considering the taint of Ida's misdeeds still remained. He knew Sydney had loved that house before all the bad stuff happened and it was his goal to build her another house similar to the style she adored, even bigger and better.

It was Sydney who suggested they move closer to his family, which had humbled Giovanni. She was such an amazing woman and he was thankful to have her in his life. He was so glad she got along so well with his brothers and their bloodmates.

He and Sydney were currently staying with Maggie and GianMarco for a brief visit because the family had decided to have an impromptu party to celebrate Dante's and Isis's good news. Isis was expecting, and both she and Dante were extremely pleased. Giovanni grinned whenever he saw Dante strut around with his chest puffed out, proud that he had created life. Giovanni couldn't wait for that to happen with him and Sydney but he realized that these things would happen in their own time. Besides, she was still getting used to being a vampire.

"As long as they're happy, I think that's all that matters," Giovanni finally answered. He looked down at his cards. He tossed his hand down with resignation. Poker was definitely not his game, but he enjoyed spending this time with his brothers.

Romeo grinned. "You're absolutely right. Because when Christine is happy, little Romeo is *very* happy."

Niccolo rolled his eyes, also tossing in his hand. "Must you always be so vulgar? Besides, your daughter is standing right behind you." Niccolo nodded in Adrienne's direction. The child had come out of nowhere. She was so tiny and cute, but sneaky like a ninja as Romeo would always joke.

Romeo's face turned bright red. He swerved in his chair to face his four year old. "Yes, *bella*?"

"Come play with me." She looked up at her father with big brown eyes. It was clear to see how the little girl had Romeo wrapped around her little finger.

"Okay, *bambina*. Daddy will be with you shortly." He gently swatted her on the bottom to send her on her way.

Adrienne skipped away.

Romeo threw in his cards on the table. "I guess I'm out, fellas. I'm off to play another rousing game of *Pretty Pretty Princess.*"

The men began to snicker, probably thinking about the picture Christine had taken of Romeo wearing a tiara and a feather boa while sitting at a tiny table with Adrienne, drinking out of tiny tea cups. Giovanni thought it was adorable, but it did make him chuckle to see his rough and gruff brother brought down by a precocious toddler.

"I think I'm going to call it in too. Gianna should be getting up from her nap soon and I'm going to go check in on her." GianMarco pushed away from the table.

Giovanni never imagined he'd see this day when he and his younger brothers could be laughing together and simply be a family. It made him realize that everything he did to keep them safe had not been in vain. Though he had Sydney by his side for which he'd be forever thankful, he had something else, just as important.

He had family.

## About the Author

NYT and USA Today Bestselling Author Eve has always enjoyed creating characters and stories from an early age. As a child she was always getting into mischief, so when she lost her television privileges (which was often), writing was her outlet. Her stories have gotten quite a bit spicier since then! When she's not writing or spending time with her family, Eve is reading, baking, traveling or kicking butt in 80's trivia. She loves hearing from her readers. She can be contacted through her website at: www.evevaughn.com.